## JESSIE'S IN HOT WATER...

Jessie locked the door, undressed, and tested the water in the copper tub. She was about to step into the water when the first shot came.

She flung herself down as a fusillade shattered the tub and water streamed out!

There were perhaps ten shots, every one slamming into the copper tub, inches above her head. Then silence. She lifted herself slowly, staring at the round holes in the copper sides. Someone had tried to kill her!

WESLEY ELLIS

# LONE STAR
## AND THE
## GAMBLE OF DEATH

JOVE BOOKS, NEW YORK

LONE STAR AND THE GAMBLE OF DEATH

A Jove Book/published by arrangement with
the author

**PRINTING HISTORY**
Jove edition/January 1990

ISBN: 0-515-10213-X

Jove Books are published by The Berkley Publishing Group,
200 Madison Avenue, New York, New York 10016.
The name "Jove" and the "J" logo
are trademarks belonging to Jove Publications, Inc.

PRINTED IN THE UNITED STATES OF AMERICA

10  9  8  7  6  5  4  3  2  1

# Chapter 1

Dutch Bradshaw rode around the low hills and halted on a rise that overlooked the steel rails. It was evening; the sun had gone and the western sky was a riot of flame that slowly subsided. The air was very clear and the light was sufficient for Dutch to see the several buildings that clustered about the water tower.

There was a line of shacks, three or four, probably used by maintenance crews. Near the tower was a sod and stone house with a log roof that probably housed the permanent resident and his family, the man in charge of the tower. Dutch could see no telegraph shack and he smiled grimly. That didn't matter. He and the boys would cut the wires a couple of miles from the tower.

He watched lights come on in the stone house, yellow and glimmering. Smoke rose from the chimney, a tall gray column in the still air. They were probably having supper down there. . . .

Turning the horse, Dutch rode south. He was to meet the others at Frypan Creek. He studied the sky. They should have arrived there late that afternoon, six of them, up from Winder's Place on the Red River. It shouldn't take more than seven men to do the job.

Dutch reached the camp in less than three hours to find most of the men asleep. Howie was awake, expecting him. Howie was as lean and tall as Dutch. "Thought you'd got lost."

"You save me any coffee?"

"Made you a pot fresh. There's some beef, too. How'd the tower look to you?"

The two men sat at the tiny fire. Dutch filled a tin cup with coffee and sipped it. "Just like the last time we looked. Didn't see no changes."

"Good." Howie dished up some beef stew and passed it across to the other. "When d'we hit it?"

"Tomorrow when the train gets there. Supposed to be the middle of the afternoon. We'll cut the wires at noon and be waitin' for the train."

Howie nodded.

They rode north the next morning, and when they reached the tracks, Howie pointed to the telegraph wires, and the men whooped and fired six-guns, smashing insulators, pulling down the wires. Repair crews would have to start from each end and work toward the break. It might take them several days to find it.

They followed the rails five miles farther on, to the water tank. A lone, older man was chopping wood near the stone house and they ran him inside: "Stay there."

Then they waited for the westbound train.

Two hours later they heard its whistle, far down the

2

track. It came pounding in, shushing steam and coal smoke, and halted by the water tower.

Each of Dutch's men had a specific job. Two of them took the engineer and fireman off the cab and put them into the stone house with orders to stay put: "Do as you're told and nobody gets hurt."

Dutch led two men into the first baggage car. The others kept the passengers on the train. The baggage car held luggage and freight. When the door of the second car opened, Dutch, with a pistol in each hand, opened fire. Three Pinkertons were shot at once. A fourth guard with a shotgun got off a blast into the ceiling before he was cut down.

They had achieved complete surprise. Dutch had expected more than four guards, but the raid had gone exactly as planned. The four bodies were laid on the ground outside, then the passengers were herded off the train and most of the luggage tossed off. Planks were found to form a ramp, and the seven horses were put aboard the baggage car.

With one of the raiders in the cab, the train moved out. The raid had taken less than three quarters of an hour.

Colonel Marshall Harrison, commandant of Nebraska Territory's Fort Gillespie, was an old Civil War buddy of Jessica Starbuck's father. They were, in fact, both major generals in that war—and had reverted to permanent rank after it was over.

Harrison had received the reports from Pinkertons and from law enforcement groups in the area of the train robbery-murders, and was dissatisfied with all of them. He sat in his office and shuffled through them looking for some indication that the writers of the reports knew more than the newspaper stories everybody was reading.

He was a big man, white-haired and thick about the

3

middle. Advancing age would dictate his retirement soon, but it had not affected his brain in the least. Something was very smelly in this affair—it smelled of incompetence. An entire train had disappeared and none of the lawmen could find it!

Harrison got up and stood at the window. An entire train! How the hell could a train disappear into thin air?

Along with the army payroll!

Some smart crook had burned the midnight oil on this one, figuring angles. Had he attached balloons and flown the damned thing off into the hills? Was that possible? Some of the more imaginative newspaper reporters were suggesting that it had been buried beside the tracks after the money sacks had been removed.

But it would take a regiment to bury a train engine and cars! And even so, a regiment would take a week to do it. This affair had taken no time at all, apparently. Repair crews had gone out in two directions seeking the break in the telegraph wire and had discovered the crime at the water tower. It had taken only a day and a half.

And all the reports said the train had disappeared. Would it be possible to camouflage it somehow? Harrison shook his head. One car, maybe, but not a train.

Could it have been dismantled? He sighed and shook his head again. As foolish an idea as burying it.

Maybe his balloon idea would work after all. How many balloons would it take to lift the enormous weight of a train engine? He had no idea. He was not an engineer, but he suspected there were not that many balloons in existence.

No, the train simply had to be somewhere no one had yet looked. Except that the reports said they had looked everywhere.

Obviously they had not.

He had instructed his adjutant, Major Jennings, to make arrangements for a second payroll delivery. And in the meantime he had wired Jessica Starbuck in Kansas City, asking if she could make the journey to Fort Gillespie.

Her return wire said she would be there in ten days or less. She had a bit of business to wind up.

Five days later the second payroll, which had been sent by stagecoach, had been ambushed, the guards and driver killed.

Colonel Harrison pounded his desk. How could this happen!? Major Jennings wrung his hands. "Every precaution had been taken! Secrecy had been absolute! Not even the guards knew what they were guarding!"

"Somebody knew," Harrison growled. "It's no damned coincidence! Check out every man again."

"Yes, sir." Jennings ran out.

★

# Chapter 2

Jessica Starbuck followed Ki off the stagecoach in Hanover . . . the nearest town to Fort Gillespie a mile distant. She was instantly the center of all eyes, a honey-blond, green-eyed lady in a modest navy-blue traveling suit over a white blouse.

Her full breasts bobbed pleasantly as she stepped down to the dusty street. No one looked at the slim man by her. He wore a cotton shirt under a leather vest, and his black jeans were molded to sinuous thighs. His dark eyes darted here and there under the wide brim of a flat Stetson, and if anyone had looked at him they might have wondered what he was. He certainly was not Indian . . . he might have been Mexican . . . or Oriental, but he had no pigtail.

However, he pulled their luggage off the stage, crooked his finger at a boy, offering him a dime to tote their bags into the hotel across the street. Then he followed the blond woman, smiling to himself at the attention she aroused.

Colonel Harrison had arranged rooms for them at the Hanover Hotel and her first task was to send a message to him that they had arrived.

A messenger sought her out in the dining room that evening as she and Ki enjoyed a supper with candlelight and wine for the first time since leaving Kansas City. The message said that Colonel Harrison would send an escort in the morning to bring her and Ki—whom he knew about—to the fort.

Ki hired a four-wheeled rig with a top from the livery stable, and when the escort, five men and a young fresh-faced lieutenant whose eyes widened at sight of Jessie, showed up, they set out. The lieutenant whisked them through the guard gate and across a parade ground that was lined with whitewashed stones. They halted in front of an imposing building with a carefully lettered legend above the wide door: POST COMMANDER.

Ki gave her his arm as she stepped down and Colonel Harrison hurried from the building, "My dear Jessica! It is so good to see you!"

The lieutenant and his men snapped to attention and the colonel led her up the steps and into the cool building, chatting busily—ignoring everyone else.

In his spacious office he shook Ki's hand and asked them to be seated. And in a moment a sergeant came in with a tray containing biscuits, wine, and glasses. He set it on a small table between them and hurried out, closing the door softly.

The colonel said, "Jessica, I know what you've done in the past, you and Ki, and I hope you can help us. We are about at the end of our rope—so to speak."

"Are you referring to the payroll robberies and the murders the newspapers are having a field day about?"

7

"Yes, I am. Is there any way I can enlist your services in this matter? The Starbuck empire is suffering, too, you know. The Star Jay Company could be in very grave trouble—"

"Of course we'll help you," Jessie said, glancing at Ki, who nodded. "Why don't you tell us about it."

"Where shall I start!"

"At the beginning. Tell us what happened at the water tank. Were there any witnesses?"

"Yes, several—in the house. There was a house for the man who tended the water tank—this was one of those rare situations where the water tank was far from a town. The raiders, seven of them, put him into the house, then waited for the westbound train to arrive. I have all the reports here if you'd like to read them."

Jessie shook her head. "You tell us."

"The seven men waited for the train, and when it arrived they hustled the crew and the passengers off, and one of the seven got into the cab and the train moved out and that's the last anyone's seen of it. It disappeared into thin air."

Ki asked, "Were any of the raiders recognized?"

"No. We don't know who they were. The army has offered a two thousand dollar reward, and so has the railroad. They'd like their train back."

Jessie asked, "How much did they get? Are the newspaper stories accurate?"

"Yes. They got thirty-five thousand dollars in cash in both robberies. As you probably know, the army pays off in cash at the end of every month."

"A total of seventy thousand dollars . . ."

"Yes." Harrison nodded. "A great deal of money. And there will be a third shipment necessary." His big fists clenched. "We've been sending the payroll the same way

8

for years, and this is the first time—the first two times—we've been robbed."

Jessie said, "We'd like to go out to the water tank and look at the actual land. . . ."

Colonel Harrison rose and went to the wall. His finger tapped a large map. "The money started from here." He put his finger on a town, then followed a heavy line. "This is the railroad, about three hundred miles to the water tank. We call it Tank one-oh-two." His finger moved on. "The next town is Grainton, and the train never reached it." He tapped the map. "Somewhere between Grainton and one-oh-two, it went up in smoke."

Ki asked, "Is there anything special between one-oh-two and Grainton?"

The colonel shook his head. "I don't think so. . . . Would you like me to arrange an escort for you?"

"No," Jessie said. "We'd rather go there on our own."

"Very well. But please call on me for anything—we are most anxious to clear this matter up—I mean, catch the crooks and recover the money."

"Of course," Jessie said.

As they were leaving, Major Jennings appeared, a smallish, prim-looking man with a cheery smile. He had orders from the commanding officer, he told them, to put the post's resources at their command.

"Wire me," he said, "and whatever you wish will be done—if it is possible under the sun."

They thanked him and went out to the rig. The young lieutenant and his men were waiting and whirled them back to the hotel in town.

Water tower 102 was exactly as the colonel had described it, a desolate spot in the middle of nowhere. They took the train to Grainton, a depot town with several sidings, a telegraph office, and a single main street, dusty and rutted.

A restaurant put up food for them, and the livery stable provided horses and canteens. Jessie changed into shirt and jeans, strapped on a Colt pistol, and they set out, following the steel rails.

Jessie said, "How does a train disappear?"

"A train can't disappear . . . not for very long. Somehow it's been overlooked."

She laughed. "How can you overlook anything as big as a train engine and passenger cars?"

Ki shrugged. "What if it *was* buried?"

"You heard what the colonel said about that. . . ."

"Yes, but what if there was a big enough ditch beside the tracks—I mean already there—and they simply put the train into it."

She looked at him. "Simply *put* the train into it? Sort of pushed it over?"

Ki chuckled. "It is a foolish idea. All right. We agree the train wasn't buried, right?"

"Exactly."

"So it has got to be somewhere, sitting, waiting for us. But it has to be on rails." Ki gestured at the desert about them. "You couldn't push a train one inch in this sand."

"You're saying it's on a siding?"

He shrugged again. "Doesn't it have to be?"

"But every siding has already been investigated."

"Not by us," Ki said.

The rails led eastward, occasionally curving gently around a hill or avoiding a steep depression, but for the most part pointing east as if drawn by a straightedge. No siding led away from them.

But as they approached tank 102, perhaps ten miles from it, they came on a branch line. There was a switch,

10

heavily padlocked, and rails that curved north into the emptinesses.

"No one told us about this," Jessie said, shading her eyes as she peered into the shimmering distance.

"Possibly because it's been investigated thoroughly and nothing found."

"Is that good enough?"

Ki nudged his horse. "All right. We'll check it out—but there will be no train."

It took them two days to reach the end of the branch line. It halted at a wide dry wash. The tracks simply ended and there were none on the far side of the wash.

There had been a town or settlement of some kind at the end of the track, a large area had been dragged and leveled, and there were still many evidences of building foundations. It was common for mining towns to build up, some almost overnight, and fold the same way, everything loaded on flat cars and hauled to the next strike.

Ki pointed out old mines in the hills nearby. "When the ore played out, they moved on."

"And no train," Jessica said with a sigh. "Why didn't they pull the rails up?"

"They probably will, one day."

They retraced their steps and went on to tank 102, reaching it at dusk, several days later. The man in charge was Hiram Wiggins, a man of about sixty years who told them he had worked for the railroad all his life.

"But I never been so scared as when them men come here and helt up the train."

"Would you recognize any of them if you saw them again?" Ki asked.

"Maybe. I was scared they'd do harm to the old lady— you know."

11

"But they didn't?"

"They just run me into the house. Never looked at her."

"How long were they here?"

"Maybe two hours, waitin' for the westbound. They stayed out by the tank there. They killed the Pinkertons—I heard the shootin', then they moved the train out."

"D'you have any idea where it went?"

Wiggins laughed. "Some folks says in the paper they buried it."

"What do *you* think they did with it?"

The older man shook his head. "I got no damn idea atall. If they could git it past Grainton, there's lots of places they might take it."

"*Past* Grainton," Jessie said, looking at Ki. "Could they have gotten it past Grainton?"

"Nope," Wiggins said, "lessen ever'body there was asleep. A train makes a passel of noise. Woulda woke 'em up. They'd have to be drugged or dead."

Jessie mused, "I wonder if anyone thought of that?"

"We'll ask when we get back," Ki said.

# Chapter 3

There was no room for them in the small stone house, but behind it was a deep depression, grassy and pleasant under cottonwood trees. It was the place where the train's passengers had been herded, according to Hiram Wiggins.

"It was a cold day, as I r'member. Them people all huddled together down there and made 'em some fires to keep warm."

"And no one was hurt but the Pinkertons?" Jessie asked.

Wiggins nodded vigorously. "They was killers, miss. We all knew it and none of us wanted to take no chances. We done just like they told us. They fired a lot of shots in the air when they made them folks go down there. It was like a goddam Fourth of July for a spell."

After Wiggins left them it was full dark. Ki had a fire going in moments, and they made a supper and boiled coffee.

Jessie said, "How do you make a train disappear?"

Ki laughed. He waved his hands, "Abracadabra—now you see it, now you don't."

"I'm serious. There has to be an answer."

"It went through Grainton at night when everyone was asleep, as Wiggins said."

She regarded him. "Do you believe that?"

"No." He sighed. "I don't see how it's possible. As Wiggins said, a train makes a lot of noise—and they were expecting it."

Jessica nodded. She rose and walked about the grassy plot. From where they were, they could not see the stone house or the tower. She stared at the hillside.

"Ki—"

"Yes?"

She went back to the fire. "The train never reached Grainton. That's what everyone says."

He nodded. "What're you getting at?"

"The colonel, the newspapers, everyone—they all say the train disappeared between here, tower one-oh-two, and Grainton. Isn't that so?"

"Yes . . ."

"Ki," she paused, staring at him, "what if it went the other way?"

"What?"

"What if—instead of going toward Grainton—it backed up, going the other way?"

"Yi yi yi," Ki said, momentarily startled.

She pointed. "You can't see the tower from here—so the people herded down here couldn't see the train, either. They heard it leave—that's all. They assumed it went toward Grainton."

"But—Wiggins in the stone house—"

"Where are the windows in that house?"

14

Ki rose abruptly. "High up—the house was built as a fort!"

"So maybe no one saw the train leave. It would be out of sight in a few minutes—heading east!"

Ki took a long breath. "I think that opens up a whole new vista. The train was headed west so everyone assumed it would go on west. . . ."

"What's the next town east?"

"If I remember, it's a long way, probably two hundred miles. And we know it didn't reach that town, either, or the newspapers would have had the story." He looked at her. "So it disappeared somewhere east of here."

They set out in the morning, at first light, and rode all day without seeing anything to arouse their suspicions. A west-bound train passed them in the middle of the morning, then nothing the rest of the day.

Near the end of the second day they came to a siding that curved off to the south. The switch was padlocked and rusty, and the rails, a short distance from the main tracks, were covered over with dirt. The maintenance road they followed rode up over the earth-covered tracks and continued on. The siding looked as if it had not been used for years.

A dozen miles past the old siding they came onto a crossing. Tracks from another railway crossed at right angles and disappeared into the distances.

Halting, they studied it. Jessie said, "There's no way a train could get off one set of tracks and onto another—is there?"

"Certainly not." Ki paused. "Not without a big crane to lift the engine and cars."

"A big crane?"

He nodded. "When trains derail and wind up in the

15

ditch, big cranes lift them up and put them on the tracks again."

"So it *is* possible."

Ki shrugged. "I suppose so . . . but where would bandits get a crane?"

"Does the crane have wheels—like an engine?"

"Yes, of course. But how would bandits, even very resourceful ones, get a huge crane and an engine to pull it? All that would take enormous organization, knowledge, proper papers—it's too much. I don't believe it. And what happens to the crane after it's used?"

She smiled. "They bury it?"

Ki shook his head. "They didn't put the train on these crossing tracks. Impossible."

"You've convinced me. Let's go on."

They rode on, following the maintenance road to Kearny, and saw nothing along the way to make them pause a moment. No other train passed them in the two days it took to reach the little burg.

Kearny was the next town east from water tower 102. It had a rutted, very wide main street with only a partial boardwalk on one side. There was a huge corral next to the railway waiting room, a telegraph office and a few stores. It was weatherbeaten and poor and could not boast a hotel.

They stayed overnight and slept in the stable, bathed out of a chipped tin basin, and had breakfasts of steaks and potatoes and headed out westward two hours after sunup.

"I want to look at that siding again," Jessie said. "It's the only place a train could have gotten off the main tracks."

"But it's covered over with dirt!"

"Dirt can be shoveled."

"The switch was padlocked."

16

"Padlocks can be broken." She looked at him. "And another lock put on."

Ki scratched his chin. "Why did they go to all the trouble of stealing a train?"

"Because it has given them about three weeks, so far, to make their escape. Everybody's been looking for the train instead of the bandits."

"I suppose you're right. They could be in South America by now, spending the army's money."

Days later, when they reached the siding, Ki examined the lock on the switch. It showed signs of having been tampered with. They had no shovel, but they prodded the earth covering the siding tracks, and Ki thought it seemed softer than it should.

"It's possible the earth was shoveled off the tracks, enough so the train could pass, then shoveled back again and tamped down."

"Let's follow the tracks."

In about ten miles the rails divided, one track leading eastward, the other continuing south.

They rode east and discovered the rails stopped in about two miles at the foot of a steep outcropping. The area looked as if someone had been loading sand or gravel.

They continued south for two days.

In the middle of the morning of the third day they came on the train. "Eureka!" Ki said.

The tracks halted at the end of a long, narrow valley. They were in a region of jumbled hills where there were hundreds of old mine excavations. The engine and cars were parked at the end of the track. No one was about.

Both express cars were standing open; there was dried blood on the floor of the last car. The freight seemed untouched, but the money in the heavy cloth government sacks was gone.

They could find no clue to the raiders.

"Time to go back and report," Ki said.

"And get a real bath," Jessie agreed.

# Chapter 4

Aaron Madison was a big man, the word many used about him was *commanding*. He had a way of speaking that made his words seem carved in stone. Few stood up to him when he had that special light in his eyes.

He was a wealthy man in a place where most were poor. He was a landowner—he had vast acres and he himself did not know how many he controlled. He had only a vague idea of his boundaries—but, of course, boundaries seldom occupied his thoughts.

And his thoughts soared. He dreamed dreams that others feared even to contemplate. But his most compelling dream was one that he confided to almost no one—he planned to establish another state, named for himself, carving it out of north Texas.

His grandiose plans had only one flaw—himself. He did not realize the flaw and would not have acknowledged it had anyone dared tell him. It was that he cared nothing for the law—if the law interfered with his plans. And in that vein he really cared nothing for any law . . . not made by himself. He was above the law, and when he needed cash, his men rode great distances to get it for him.

Dutch Bradshaw was one. Dutch had brought him seventy thousand dollars.

And now he had information of a second payroll delivery, this time sent by both train and stagecoach, destination Fort Gillespie. Madison laid the information before Dutch and sent him on his way.

No one but himself knew his various informers. Madison kept it that way. He well knew how men were tempted. He paid the informers with the money he collected by their information.

Dutch Bradshaw studied the map Madison had given him. The stagecoach with the money in canvas sacks would come along this road, make a sharp turn at the bridge and head north. He would hit the stage as it slowed to make the turn. It was only necessary to shoot one of the team horses and the stage would come to a halt.

With four men he rode out to look over the ground. Howie was with him, lean and tanned as himself. Howie was a good man with a Winchester.

At the bridge Dutch said, "You wait till they slow, then you take the right-hand leader. That'll slew the stage around some."

"All right." Howie tipped his hat back and looked around at the sandy hills. Just above them might be a good place to shoot from. He pointed it out and Dutch agreed. Howie climbed up and found a ledge about fifteen feet above the road. Perfect.

Dutch said to the others, "As soon as the stage stops,

the rest of us'll make sure none of them guards gets a chance to spit."

"How many guards?"

"Prob'ly four inside the coach and one up by the driver. There won't be any reg'lar passengers." Dutch looked at each man. "You-all understand?"

They nodded, fingering rifles.

The bridge provided a good roof and they made camp under it. Two men fashioned a rope corral several hundred yards away in the tall willows where the horses could not be seen from the road.

By noon of the next day every man was in place; the stage was due.

They watched it approach from a long distance, six horses and a Concord; two men on the box. It made a wide turn to get to the bridge, and the horses slowed to a walk, climbing a slight hill. Howie poked the Winchester between two rocks and followed the lead horses.

The ambush was a complete surprise. Howie's shot was perfect. The right-hand leader went down in a swirl of dust, dead before he hit the ground. The swingers and wheelers piled up as the stagecoach overturned. The driver and shotgun jumped free, but as they rose they were hit by concentrated rifle fire. The six men were massacred.

Dutch and his men rode directly to Coopersville, east and south. They did not enter the town, but stopped in a ramshackle barn that apparently no one owned, a mile west of the town.

They waited a day, then Aaron Madison showed up, riding in a buggy with another man. It was a cold afternoon and they had built a fire in the barn. Madison warmed his hands and asked about the Concord. Dutch gave him a brief report and handed over the money sacks.

"You-all did well," Madison said. He opened the sacks and totaled the money, eighteen thousand in bills and gold. He counted out two hundred for each man and passed it around. He gave Dutch another two hundred for train fare, ordering them to Kansas City.

"Wait there for three weeks, then come back by twos and threes. The heat'll be off by then." Madison went out and got into the buggy.

Another group, headed by Willie Hobart, hit the train just out of Tulle Creek. The other half of the army payroll was supposed to be in the express car—but was not. Three men died in order for Willie to find that fact out.

Aaron Madison was enraged! His information was faulty!

His informant got back to him the following day to say there had been a last-minute change that he had not been privy to. The shipment had gone by another train. Those things happened.

Jessica and Ki rode to Grainton and wired Colonel Harrison, making a report; the train was found, but not the army payroll. The railroad authorities were notified, and a crew was sent to rescue the lost train.

The colonel sent them facts concerning the bridge massacre, asking them to look into it.

The nearest town to the site of the holdup was Timmins. They took a stagecoach there and got horses from a stable. The site of the bridge holdup was about five miles distant, and they reached it in the middle of the afternoon.

It was an ideal place for an ambush. Ki climbed the side of the hill and found several spent shell cases. Someone had probably shot the leader horse from this spot. Only one horse had been killed. The repair crew had righted the stage and taken it back to Timmins with the other five horses.

The tracks of the gang who had done the holdup were impossible to follow. They had stayed on the well traveled road.

When they returned to the army post, Ki asked Colonel Harrison if he had someone who might compare the shell cases taken from the tower 102 holdup and those he had found at the bridge.

A young lieutenant had a strong magnifying glass, and with it he determined that several of the cases had ejector marks that matched.

"That proves," Ki said, "that the same group was at both places."

"It's a conspiracy!" Harrison said angrily.

"It also proves something else," Jessie said to them.

"What?"

"That the bandits had inside information. How could they possibly know the payroll money would be on the stagecoach unless someone told them?"

"By God, that's right!" The colonel stared at her. "You mean someone here on the post?"

"It's possible. How many knew about the shipments?"

"I don't know. Let's ask Jennings." He sent for the adjutant.

Jennings arrived, hurriedly buttoning his tunic. He closed the door and clicked his heels.

The colonel said, "How many knew about the shipment of money?"

Jennings paused and checked off names on his fingers. "Eight, sir. Nine counting me."

"Nine people to keep a secret like that!?"

Jennings made a tiny shrug. "Sir, we've been sending the payroll that way for years."

23

Colonel Harrison frowned at the smaller man. "Is any one of them new?"

"Three are, sir. Three men did not reenlist. I had to fill out the group."

"How long ago?"

Jennings blinked. "About three months, sir . . . as close as I can remember. I can look it up."

Harrison glanced at Jessica. "I'll order an internal investigation at once . . . let you know how it comes out." He turned back to Major Jennings. "Send Captain Morgan into my office, please."

"Yes, sir." Jennings hurried out.

Harrison went to a sideboard and poured out drinks, handing them around. "That was a brilliant piece of work, finding the train . . . when no one else could."

"We had some luck, Colonel," Jessie said. "But where do we go from here?"

"An interesting question . . ."

Ki asked, "How are you going to send the payroll from now on, sir?"

"Well, actually that's not up to me. I'll be informed as soon as they figure it out. I'm only in charge of a post out in Nebraska Territory."

They returned to Hanover and discussed plans over supper in the restaurant. The raiders had left few clues behind. Where did one start looking for them?

A tall, good-looking man came to their table. "Excuse me . . . I'm told you are Miss Starbuck . . ."

"Yes," Jessie said.

"My name is Paul Nicholson. I'm a reporter and I wonder if you'd give me a few moments."

Jessica looked him over, glanced at Ki, and said, "Sit down, Mr. Nicholson. A few moments about what?"

Nicholson pulled out a chair and sat. "I'm told you two

were the ones who found the missing train . . . when no one else could."

"We were lucky."

The reporter smiled. "I know it was much more than that. I looked for that damned train myself. It never occurred to me that it might have gone east instead of west. What made you think that?"

"Logic, Mr. Nicholson." She indicated Ki. "My associate is Ki."

Nicholson offered his hand and they shook. "Are you Chinese, sir?"

"Half Japanese," Ki said. "Very inscrutable."

The reporter laughed. "Well, whatever. You two are the talk of the town, you know. You've done the impossible in only a few days. May I use your names in my story?"

"No, you may not. The story isn't ended yet and exposing us might do us harm."

Nicholson nodded. "Very well. I'll write it without names. Do you have any ideas about who did the murders and robberies?"

"Nothing we can discuss with a reporter." Jessie smiled to take any sting out of the words. Paul Nicholson was a very engaging young man.

Ki said, "Do you have any ideas or information about the raiders?"

"We've been talking about it—I mean the members of the press group, and we're wondering if Aaron Madison might be behind these crimes." Nicholson shrugged. "That's a wild idea, of course, completely without basis—"

Jessie asked, "Who in the world is Aaron Madison?"

Nicholson seemed surprised. "He is only one of the most powerful men in the West—in terms of money, land, and people he controls. His reputation is abominable, he is cordially hated by thousands, and it is said he will do anything to gain his ends."

Jessie smiled. "You don't care much for him. . . ."

"I've never met him. I know him only by reputation."

Ki asked, "Why should this man Madison rob trains and stagecoaches?"

"For the same reason any criminal does . . . for money. If Madison *is* behind these army payroll robberies, he has acquired many thousands—in cash. It could be his operating fund. He must have a large payroll himself."

Jessie said, "Tell us more about this man."

"I'll tell you what I know. His headquarters are somewhere near the Red River in north Texas. The rumor is that there's a town named after him. It is a fact that he runs some of the largest cattle ranches in the country. He owns a stageline and freighting line and doubtless other businesses."

"Then why would he need to rob for more money?"

"A man like Madison always needs money." Nicholson shook his dark head. "He needs cash. In the East the largest merchants and firms are constantly borrowing, paying back and borrowing again. Madison probably does that, too, but augments his income by high-profit crime—I suspect. I doubt very much if he would stoop to robbing just any train. He would have to know when a large sum is due. We—the press group—think he had inside information about the army payroll robberies."

"We think so, too," Jessie said. "But that may take some doing to trace."

"That's right," Nicholson agreed. "The inside information could very easily come from the other end—in Washington, D.C. In fact, I'm inclined to think it must. The payroll money is sent from there."

Ki said, "You must have other reasons for suspecting

Madison. Has he been involved in suspicious operations before?"

Nicholson laughed again. "Many many times. But no one has been able to convict him. In his own bailiwick he controls the law—judges and sheriffs are in his pocket. Even the government has been unable to pin him down."

"I wonder why we haven't heard about him before," Jessie said, glancing at Ki.

"Probably because his operations have usually stayed in the south, hundreds of miles from here." Nicholson made a face. "Remember, I told you, this is all supposition. He may be completely innocent."

"It's an interesting possibility," Jessie said. "I'm glad we had this talk."

"So am I," Nicholson said, smiling at her. He rose and slid the chair back. "I'll see you again. . . ." He walked rapidly from the dining room.

Jessie watched him go. "He could be right, you know. This man, Madison, hires men to do his dirty work—and if they're caught, it's their necks."

"It's happened many times before. Aaron Madison must be a very dangerous man to cross. And probably almost impossible to get to. He's probably surrounded by any number of hard cases."

"We've faced those before," Jessie said, smiling. "Shall we look into this possibility?"

"We can't afford not to. I suggest we discuss it with the colonel. He may have information we can use."

"Yes, good. We'll do it in the morning."

# Chapter 5

Colonel Harrison knew a great deal about Aaron Madison. He sat them down in his office and brought out a file. He sat opposite and smiled wryly. "I gathered what information I could on the man—in case I got transferred to that area."

Jessie said, "We've heard nothing good about him. And we've listened to suspicions that he may be behind the payroll robberies and murders."

Harrison nodded, making a face. "It wouldn't surprise me. Let me tell you what I know." He selected a paper. "The government sent agents to Madison, and they negotiated a right-of-way about two years ago. The plan was to put a railroad across part of Madison's land. Such a line would have saved hundreds of miles by going straight across rather than around." He glanced up at them. "But to this day not one yard of track has been laid."

"Why not?"

"Because armed men have driven off the track crews, killed some and wounded others, set materials on fire—in short, the government has found it impossible to hire men to do the work. No one wants to be shot down while doing the job."

Ki asked, "Why not protect them with troops?"

"They tried that. But troops cannot be everywhere. While the cavalry was patrolling, armed men raided the supply trains bringing in food and materials. It was worse than before. The local commander reported that he would need at least two regiments to guard the entire operation. The War Department did not have that many men to spare."

"And of course Aaron Madison knew nothing about it?"

The colonel shrugged. "Nothing at all. He deplored the raids, saying they were probably made by ruffians and criminals."

"There must have been more to it than that," Ki said.

"Yes. Government agents were killed. Even the U.S. marshal was gunned down—and not replaced. For a time Madison's police jailed every stranger, till the government finally withdrew. It also proved impossible to get Madison into a federal court. No one could serve him with the papers."

Jessie shook her head. "What is being done now?"

Colonel Harrison replaced the papers into his file. "As far as I know the politicians are studying the matter. I hear from friends in Washington that they do not want to use force—but in my opinion they will have to."

"So for the moment everything is calm—the eye of the storm?"

Harrison smiled. "Very apt. Yes, the eye of the storm." He rose and put the file away. "Are you two considering going there?"

29

"Yes," Jessica said. "It's our best lead."

Ki asked, "What would bring down Madison's empire?"

The colonel turned to look at him. "Madison's death. He has high-placed people to run the various enterprises, but from what we've been able to learn, none of them has Madison's special touch."

"Has he appointed a successor?"

"Not that we know about. We know he was married, but his wife died some years ago and they had no children." He came back and sat down again. "I don't have to tell you I'm sure, that to go into his territory will be very dangerous. . . . You'll be under suspicion simply because you are outsiders."

"We're used to that," Jessie said.

"Hmmm. Then when will you go?"

She glanced at Ki. "Tomorrow." Ki nodded.

Colonel Harrison provided a good map, and they studied the route. It would be possible to go much of the distance by stage, then, near the little town of Madison, they would have to go the rest of the way on horseback. The stageline did not run into the town from the north.

At the hotel in Hanover they made their preparations, arranged with the hotel cook for food packets for the stage journey, and had supper in the restaurant.

In the middle of the meal Paul Nicholson joined them. Jessie invited him to sit down, and he smiled and ordered supper with them. "I hear you were out at the fort today—did you learn anything?"

"You certainly hear a lot," Jessie said.

"I'm a reporter. I ask a lot of questions. I'm very nosy." He grinned at them. "For instance, I hear you're a friend of the fort commander."

Jessie admitted it. "He and my father were close."

"Ahhh. That explains it." He leaned forward. "Do you have any little bits of news I can use? Anything new about the holdups?"

"Nothing."

"Are you giving up the job?"

Jessica smiled at him. "We have no tidbits for the press."

"But you're leaving in the morning. . . ."

Ki said, "How do you know that?"

"The cook told me."

Jessie laughed. "You *are* nosy!"

"I'm a reporter. May I go with you?"

Ki asked, "Do you know where we're going?"

"No . . . I'm sorry to say."

"Then why do you want to go with us?"

Nicholson looked from one to the other. "Because I am sure that you are going to be a source of news. I know a little about your past deeds—a little, not much, and I have faith in you." He spread his hands. "Already you found the train when the others gave up."

Ki said, "It would be a great disadvantage to us to have a reporter recording our movements."

Jessie agreed. "Advertising is something we don't need. The more unknown we are the more effective."

Nicholson paused, rubbing his chin. "Well, then, what if I promised not to mention either of your names in connection with anything I write?"

"Would that be possible?"

The reporter grimaced. "It will make some stories almost impossible, I suppose, but maybe I can find a way around. . . . I'm sure my editor will think I've found a crystal ball with extraordinary powers."

Jessica shook her head. "I still don't think so, Mr. Nicholson."

31

"Paul. Call me Paul."

"All right, Paul." She looked at Ki, who nodded. "We don't think so. We work alone."

"Is that final?"

"I'm afraid so," Ki said. "We don't want to insult you, but—"

"But what?"

Ki sighed. "We don't want to be responsible for you—we don't want to have to care for you in an emergency."

"I'm not helpless!"

Ki asked, "Are you fast with a gun?"

"Well . . . I can shoot. . . ."

Ki smiled. "Shake hands with Jessie."

"What?" The reporter looked mystified.

"Shake hands with her."

Shrugging, Nicholson put his hand out. As he grasped Jessie's hand he found himself holding the barrel of a revolver. He had not seen her draw it. His hand flew up as if he had grabbed a snake! "What the hell!"

"You see what I mean," Ki said calmly.

Nicholson sat back, staring at the lovely blond woman in astonishment as she slid the pistol away. "H-how in the world did you do that?"

"It takes practice," Jessie said sweetly. "You, for instance, have been practicing quite a different trade."

"B-but—maybe I'm not as fast as greased lightning, but I can shoot. As I said, I'm not completely helpless."

"Nevertheless, we prefer to work alone."

Nicholson sighed deeply. "Very well." He gave them a weak smile. "Anyway, I tried."

They left the hotel very early the next morning, each carrying a valise. Ki also carried a Winchester. Jessica was in

32

shirt, coat, and jeans for traveling, and they walked toward the stage depot.

Paul Nicholson met them a short distance from the waiting room. "Good morning . . ."

It was a cool morning and few were on the street. The reporter wore his usual dark store clothes. Jessie said, "You're up early. Are you meeting someone?"

"I thought I'd give you one last chance to change your minds. My bag is in the waiting room."

"Well, you don't give up easily," Jessie said. "That's a point in your favor." She was looking into his face when she saw his eyes dart upward to fasten on something behind her. He made a quick movement inside his coat, "Look out!"

Jessie jumped into a doorway, and Ki flattened himself on the boardwalk beside a parked wagon as two shots slammed into the wagon and a third smashed splinters from the doorway. Ki pulled the reporter down.

"I saw two men on the rooftop," Nicholson said. He poked his head up, "They're not there now."

"One is," Jessie said. She fired quickly, then ducked down as another shot came from across the street.

Ki said, "Keep their heads down." He darted into the street as Jessie fired four times fast, clipping wood from roof eaves.

She said, "Did you recognize any of them?"

"No—I saw a glint of sun on metal, probably a gun barrel. Did you hit one?"

"Impossible to tell." She watched Ki who slid between two buildings, the Winchester ready. There were no other figures on the roofs, and people were coming to doorways along the street and she heard chattering.

A few sudden shots came from behind the buildings, then Ki appeared. He crossed the street to them. "They had horses waiting. I saw three, got a couple shots at them, but they got away."

"So we owe you something, Mr. Nicholson," Jessie said.

"Call me Paul."

"They would have got us in the backs," Ki said.

"They knew you would be going to the stageline this morning," Nicholson said. "Who did you tell?"

"Only Colonel Harrison." Jessie picked up her valise, and they went on to the waiting room.

"*I* knew," the reporter said. "But I didn't tell anyone. Maybe the colonel mentioned it. Maybe that inside information came from the fort after all."

"Very possible," Ki agreed. He looked at Jessie and they both nodded, thinking exactly the same thing. The attack came only after they had decided to go to Madison. Was Aaron Madison's arm that long?"

They had better assume it was.

In the waiting room they bought their tickets, and in a few minutes the town marshal showed up. He was a wiry-looking middle-aged man with a gray mustache, a leather vest, jeans, and a Colt pistol about his lean hips. He wore a circle star on the vest and approached them, touching his Stetson.

"You the folks got shot at a little bit ago?"

"Yes," Jessie said. "But we don't know who did the shooting."

"We saw three," Ki remarked. "But they got away."

The marshal shook his head. "One didn't. He got knocked offen his horse and one of my deputies hauled him in."

"Wonderful!" Jessie said. "Do you know him?"

"His name's Jess Bannion. But I never seen him afore. That name mean anything to you?"

34

"No, it doesn't. Is he badly hurt?"

"The doc is lookin' at him now. He got a bullet in the hip. He going to live all right. I'd like you folks to come down to the jail and give me some particulars, you bein' the folks that shot 'im."

"Of course."

The town jail was a stout fortlike building with heavy bars on all the windows and a thick plank door off the street. The wounded man was lying in one of the cells with the doctor and an assistant hovering over him.

Jessie and Ki answered the marshal's questions, and after a bit the doctor appeared, saying he had given the hurt man something to make him sleep. The bullet wound was very painful, and the man could not be moved or questioned for a while. He would be back in a few hours, the doctor told them, and left.

The marshal asked, "You got any idea why he shot at you-all?"

"We have a theory," Jessie said. "But we'd rather not have it published. Can we come back later and sit in on the questioning?"

The marshal nodded. "You goin' to tell me your theory?"

"Not unless you push us pretty hard. It's only a theory and might not be correct."

"I see. Well, I expect when we question 'im, we'll learn something." The marshal selected a cigar. "You leaving town?"

"Not now," Jessica said. "We'll wait and hear what Jess Bannion has to say."

# Chapter 6

According to the doctor, the wounded man would not be able to talk sensibly for at least eight hours. Not until the drug wore off. Jessie and Ki returned to the hotel with the marshal's promise that he would call them when Bannion was lucid.

Over dinner Ki asked, "What are the chances that this Bannion knows who hired him?"

"Very good, I'd think. Hanover's not a big town. He probably knows all the hard cases. . . ."

"What if he won't talk?"

"I think the marshal will see that he talks. One way or another. If we can find out who is selling information at the fort—it could lead us to Aaron Madison."

"Yes, I'm sure it will."

Jessica turned in early. If Bannion was able to name names, they might close this case quickly and get back to Kansas City. She slid into bed and was asleep at once.

Hours later she woke—not at all sure what had awakened her. She sat up in bed, vaguely disturbed—and in a few minutes someone rapped on her door.

Sliding out, she grasped her revolver. "Who is it?"

"Ki. Open the door."

She slid a robe about her shoulders and unlocked the door. Ki came in quickly. "Did you hear the explosion?"

"Something woke me . . ."

"Get dressed. I think it was the jail."

She stared at him. "The jail!?"

"I haven't been outside. I can't be positive, but I suspect so." He went to the door. "I'll be downstairs." He went out and she tossed the robe off. An explosion at the jail! Dynamite! Had someone tried to kill the witness?

She dressed quickly, strapped on the Colt pistol, and hurried down to the street. A few people were gathering, chattering, some running toward the jailhouse.

The explosion had apparently rocked the town. Many people had lanterns, but even without them it was apparent the jail was demolished. Ki appeared and took her elbow, steering her to one side.

"I've been around behind it. There were two explosions at the same time. Whoever was inside is dead."

"They killed Bannion!"

"Yes. Someone did. They obviously didn't want him to talk to us."

"Damn!"

"Let's get back to the hotel. We're too good targets here in the street."

The entire town was roused. When they reached the hotel, it was close to dawn, but the hotel manager had the cook up and serving coffee. Around them, people speculated on why the jail had been bombed. Jessie and Ki sat in the dining room with a pot of coffee, listening to the chatter.

Paul Nicholson came downstairs, dressed as usual in a dark suit. When he saw them he came to the table. "What's this all about?"

Jessie said, "Sit down and have some coffee."

"I heard the jail was blown up."

"Yes, it was. Someone killed our witness."

Nicholson swore under his breath. "This is getting close to home. Whoever did that probably knows you two are on the case! You could be next."

"Yes. That has occurred to us," Ki said.

"Who else was in the jail?"

"We don't know."

Nicholson got up. "I'd better find out. My editor will want all the facts." He gulped down half a cup of coffee and hurried out to the street.

He returned half an hour later. "The marshal was home in bed, but one of his deputies..." He shrugged. "He never knew what happened. There was no one else in the jail but Bannion, and the entire jail was leveled."

Later that day they had a message from Colonel Harrison expressing his dismay over the jail bombing. His investigation, so far, had turned up no one. He would intensify it.

The next day they prepared to board the stage, and Paul Nicholson insisted on going along. There was no way they could prevent his buying a ticket, and so he boarded the Concord with them, smiling at Jessica.

There were four other passengers, all men who stared at the honey-blonde and who stumbled over themselves at every stop to help her down or give her a seat.... She always smiled prettily at them as Ki and the reporter exchanged looks. If they only knew. . . .

The first day they lost one passenger and gained another, a much older man who could not take his eyes off Jessica. Each night they slept in tiny rooms or cubicles in the way stations. Jessie reported that the older man had come to her room at night and begged her to let him in. Nicholson was annoyed and would have taken the man aside, but Ki only laughed, saying Jessie could more than take care of herself.

In three days they came to Telamond, a town named after a founding father who had once been elected to Congress. It was a small burg but busy, a river town with much traffic.

They got off the stagecoach and took rooms in the Delmart Hotel. There had been no possibility of a bath in any of the way stations, and Jessie was determined to have one . . . as well as a decent meal.

The bathhouse was behind the hotel and divided into two parts, male and female. Male patrons made their own fires for hot water, but the hotel charged a dime extra for females because a boy stoked the fire and poured the hot water into the large copper tub for them.

Jessie locked the door when the boy had gone, undressed, and tested the water. The tub had a wooden seat and back so that patrons did not scald themselves. She was about to step into the water when the first shot came.

She flung herself down as a fusillade shattered the tub and water streamed out.

There were perhaps ten shots, every one slamming into the copper tub, inches above her head. Then silence. She lifted herself slowly, staring at the round holes in the copper sides. Someone had tried to kill her!

She dressed quickly, and there was a loud rapping on

the door. When she opened it the hotel manager and Ki came in, both vastly relieved to see her unhurt.

The manager sputtered apologies, and Ki went out to the alley behind the bathhouse. Someone had stood there with a rifle and sent the shots through the thin wall, into the tub. There was a splash of black paint on the outer wall, and all the shots had gone through it.

When he took Jessie aside, Ki said, "This was carefully planned. Someone saw us come into the hotel . . ."

"And figured I'd want a bath."

"Yes. There was a mark on the outside wall of the bathhouse so the shooter knew where to aim. If your reflexes weren't so good, you'd be Swiss cheese now."

"But I still want a bath."

"I'll arrange it with the manager to let you use the other side. And Paul and I will use it, too."

The manager had no objections. He would have to send East for another copper tub. . . .

Ki stood guard while Jessie bathed, then he and Paul took turns at the tub, and they went into the hotel dining room. Paul was still shaken by the event.

"I think you should give up this case—it's too dangerous!"

Jessica was surprised. "Give it up!?"

"But there have already been two attempts on your lives that I know about!"

"We never give up a case," Ki said quietly.

"But—but—"

Jessie smiled, patting the reporter's hand. "We know the odds against us, Paul. They're acceptable."

"But—someone could come into this dining room in the next moment and—"

Ki said, "There are two doors. I'm facing one and Jessie

is facing the other. It's unlikely that anyone could get off a shot."

Nicholson took a long breath. "I've never met anyone like either of you!" He sighed deeply. "I see that nothing I say will make a difference."

"I'm afraid not," Ki agreed.

# Chapter 7

Telamond was only about eighty miles from Madison, according to the map they consulted in the hotel office. And the stage did not go there.

"Nobody goes there," the hotel manager said. "That's Aaron Madison's country. People *leave* there—if they can."

"What d'you mean, if they can?" Nicholson asked.

"If they can afford to leave. Madison owns the stores and the banks, and just about everything else. If you get into debt with him, you pay hell getting out."

"We'll just be passing through," Ki said. He took Jessie aside. "We'd better buy ourselves a couple of horses and take a roundabout route."

"Across country?"

"Yes. They'll expect us on the road."

"I wish I knew who 'they' were."

"So do I. But we may find out soon. What about Paul?"

Jessie shook her head. "For his own good maybe we should leave him behind."

"Yes, I think so. Just being seen with us would probably mark him. He'd have no chance against hired gunmen. We can slide out before sunup. All right?"

"Yes."

The local livery stable had a dozen horses for sale, and they selected two good-looking bays, bought used saddles, bridles, and saddlebags, and took the saddlebags back to the hotel.

Remembering that Paul Nicholson had squeezed information from a hotel cook, Ki went down the street to a restaurant and bought food for the journey.

Settling their bill the night before, they left the hotel long before dawn and rode south following the stage road until it curved west. They went across country into a hilly area of blackjack oaks, and the weather turned cold, with a stiff wind that cut through them.

That night they made camp in the shelter of a short cliff with a tiny stream nearby, and in the morning the clouds were gone and the wind with them. The sun came out, warming the hills, and when they came to the river, it sparkled on the water.

They had to ride east for miles, until they came to a ford, marked by a wide cattle crossing. On the far side they followed a road that led away from the ford. Late in the afternoon they left the road and bent south again. By evening they halted, seeing lights ahead.

"That's Madison," Ki said. "You think we should go in tonight?"

Jessie considered. "If word has reached here from the fort—I'd say no."

"We'd better assume it has."

"Then let's wait."

They made camp miles from the town and south of it. If they rode into town the next morning would they meet opposition? Would anyone talk to them? Their chances of talking to Aaron Madison himself, Ki thought, were a million to one. If he had a home they had no idea where it was.

Their suspicions of Madison were that—only suspicions. But if he or his men attempted to do them harm, then they could be reasonably sure Madison was involved in the payroll incidents.

It was what they had come to find out.

In the morning they rode into the small town from the south, walking their horses. Madison looked like any two-bit cowtown, and smelled like one.

But as they came into the wide main street, they seemed to generate more than casual interest. Was it because strangers were rare?

Ki said, "I think someone's expecting us."

"I'm afraid so. . . ."

"If we're challenged, let's separate fast. You go left and I'll go right. They might not expect that. We can meet later where we slept last night."

"Right." Jessie nodded. "And there's the welcoming committee."

Two men stepped into the street a dozen yards in front of them. Both were beefy, wearing vests, jeans, and cartridge belts with stars pinned to them. Obviously the local law.

As they halted the older of the two said, "You-all from Telamond?"

Jessie smiled sweetly. "Is that any of your business, sir?" They both stared at her. "We are law-abiding citizens."

"We got to ast you some questions."

44

Ki said, "Are you charging us with something?"

"Dammit, ain't chargin' you with nothin'. Now git down like I said."

"Why?" Jessie asked.

The older man roared, "Because I'm the goddam law!" He went for his pistol.

Ki yelled, drawing and firing as his bay horse reared suddenly, hooves kicking. Both men jumped back, and Jessie fired over their heads.

The younger man went to one knee, leveling his pistol, and Jessie snapped a shot at his thigh as she galloped past. He rolled in the dirt.

Each of them galloped off in opposite directions, firing back, the slugs tearing up the dirt of the street. The older man emptied his Colt at the fast-disappearing Ki, who galloped between two buildings, gaining the open. The .45 slug smashed a storefront.

The entire altercation had taken only seconds. Both horses were out of sight, and one man was down in the street, holding his bloody leg.

The older man, Hedley Wade, town marshal by appointment, was disgusted when he talked later to Dutch Bradshaw. "They answered the description, a blond woman and a Chinaman. And they had us figgered in a second. The woman shot Verne in the goddam leg and I'm jest lucky they didn't shoot me."

"You're a lucky fool," Dutch agreed. "Them two're poison. Next time—if you get a next time—you shoot first. Don't give 'em a chance."

"I will."

Dutch rolled a brown cigarette and licked the flap. "You say they separated—went in opposite directions?"

"That's right. I didn't figger that."

"Uh-huh. It means they had it set aforehand what they was going to do." He struck a match. "Mr. Madison, he ain't going to like none of this."

"Do you hafta tell 'im?"

Dutch looked annoyed. "Jesus, of course. If he found out I didn't tell 'im—there'd be hell to pay. You know that."

Wade grunted. He knew.

Dutch left the marshal's office, mounted his horse, and rode out of town. Old Hedley was probably getting too ancient for the job. He didn't know where the two had gone; he hadn't stopped or detained them as his orders said. And his deputy was laid up in bed with a busted leg. Hedley had bungled it.

And too many things had been bungled lately, Dutch knew. Thank God he hadn't been responsible for any. His assignments had come off smoothly, but he still felt nervous about facing Aaron Madison. The man was unpredictable—and ruthless. No telling what he might think or do. It was well known he hated bad news.

Aaron wanted the girl and the Chinaman dead. And no one had been able to accomplish it—so far.

Dutch was certain the two were not swimming in luck. They were both quick as sidewinders and could figure ahead, anticipating trouble—as they had with Hedley Wade. None of that had been luck.

Of course, Hedley had been stupid . . . and they had taken quick advantage of it.

Dutch turned into the road that led up the long hill. Aaron Madison had built a fort on top of the hill in the trees. It was common knowledge that Aaron feared a sniper's bullet. He was aware that people hated him, and he lived in the worry that one of them would get him in a

Winchester's sights. He did everything he could to make that as difficult as possible.

As he approached the main gate, he could see the guards gather on the firestep over it. Dutch waved and yelled his name. In a moment one of the gates opened and he rode through, exchanging a few words with the guards.

He got down in front of the main house, built of stone mostly. Thousands of stones had been hauled up the hill from the creeks down below. Two riflemen were sitting by the front door. One said, "Howdy, Dutch. He expectin' you?"

Dutch nodded and they passed him in. He dropped his hat onto a hattree and went along a hall to the office. The door was open and he paused. Aaron sat across the room, behind his big teak desk with a Colt pistol in front of him. Willie Hobart sat to the right, grinning, and Dutch nodded to both.

Madison said, "Come on, Dutch. Willie, get him something."

"No, thanks," Dutch said, and Willie sat back down.

"What is it?" Madison asked.

"Them two, the blond girl and the Chinaman, came into town this morning."

Madison snapped his fingers. "Go on—"

"Hedley let 'em get away."

The big man behind the desk frowned. "What happened?"

"They rode in and Hedley and Verne stopped them in the street. There was some quick gunplay, and the two of 'em rode out fast. Verne took one in the leg. Hedley don't know where they went."

Madison ground his teeth together. He took a long breath, staring out the near window. He had heavy black brows and lank hair. His jowls were thick and his hands

47

pudgy. He dressed in a black store suit with a silver chain across his middle.

He said softly, "We'll have to put someone in Hedley's place." He looked at Willie. "Think on it."

"All right."

"What's your opinion, Dutch?"

"Well, we don't know what them two're doing here." He shrugged. "What can they do?"

"Cause trouble," Willie said.

Dutch made a face. "We can handle any trouble they cause. I guess we better hunt 'em down."

Madison nodded. "Exactly. Hunt 'em down. I'm putting you in charge of that, Dutch. You take what men you need and get the job done. I want them both buried out there in the hills somewhere. And don't mark the graves." Madison snapped his fingers again. "There's a bonus in it for you when it's done."

# Chapter 8

Aaron Madison was going to be a tough nut to crack. If the Federal Government could not bring him to justice, how would they manage it? They met at the camping site and could not formulate a plan.

"We simply don't know enough about him," Jessie said.

"And we can't get close without being shot at." Ki was doubtful. "Even if one of us could get into the town, would anyone talk to us—I mean, tell us what we need to know about Madison?" He made a gesture of futility. "They're probably all afraid to talk to strangers."

"Yes, probably. But he must live somewhere—maybe we can find out where."

"It'd be heavily guarded. Besides, what good would it do to talk to him? And it would certainly be impossible to abduct him. . . ."

Jessica sighed deeply. "There must be a way."

"Remember Colonel Harrison said there was a way—use the army. I'm beginning to think he's right."

"It takes preparation to organize a military operation and get it moving, and if Madison has a spy at the fort, giving him information . . ." Jessica shrugged, making a wry face. "That would hardly work, either. He would hear about it long before."

"Yes, that's right," Ki said glumly.

They were sitting the horses near a clump of trees a mile or so from the town, and Ki's eye was caught by movement. He nudged Jessica. A group of men rode out at a walk, heading north.

She shaded her eyes. "It looks like a posse."

"I suppose they're after us."

Jessie smiled. "I'm sure they'd like to have us in their jail."

"Yes. Then they'd burn it down."

There were seven men in the group, and as they left the town behind, they began to straggle, with the leader far out in front.

Ki fished in his saddlebags for binoculars and trained them on the distant riders.

"They certainly look like a posse. . . ." He handed the glasses to Jessica.

She focused them. "They're halting." In another moment she said, "They're all looking this way and one's pointing." She gave the glasses back. "I think they've seen us."

Ki studied the horsemen for several moments, then nodded and slipped the binocs back into the saddlebags. "They've seen us all right. Probably a flash of light on metal. We'd best make tracks. They're too many guns for us."

50

Turning, they rode eastward at a lope. In a few minutes Jessie looked back. The horsemen were coming after them.

They rode steadily for an hour, pointing mostly northeast, and their pursuers were dogged. They did not gain, but they were not shaken off. The weather remained fair and sunny—they would have preferred a storm—and the land was hilly but easy to traverse . . . and they were leaving an easy trail to follow.

They crossed a number of small streams, each time following the stream in the water for a short distance, hoping the pursuers would pause to make sure which direction they had gone, and apparently they did.

Toward evening Ki said, "We may be far enough ahead to double back."

Jessie agreed. "Let's look for a good spot. . . ."

They found it in a rocky area where the horses' hooves left little or no trace on the ground. They went past it half a mile, then turned back and raced to the rocky flat and moved off at right angles. As they left the hard-packed area, Ki got down and brushed out all evidences of their passing for fifty or sixty yards.

"By the time they find the right trail—if they do find it," Ki said, "it'll be dark."

They rode on, making a big swing toward the west. They had decided to return to Hanover and report to Colonel Harrison. They needed a new plan of attack on Aaron Madison and his empire. If one could be found.

They came out of the hilly region toward dawn, having ridden most of the night, picking their way slowly, hoping their pursuers were also in unfamiliar country.

But they were not, apparently. In the morning, as they crossed a dry wash, Ki spotted horsemen off to their left.

51

The binocs showed seven men. "Damn!" Ki said. "They outguessed us."

The day became a long chase with the pursuers gaining very little. However, they became widely separated, only two men in the lead began to close with Jessie and Ki as the afternoon progressed.

Their mounts were tiring, and Ki suggested they stop and discourage the two behind them before the animals were worn out. Jessica agreed.

They were on the undulating prairie, and Ki selected a ridge and, as they crossed it, reined in, jumping down as he yanked out his Winchester. He flopped on his belly, poking the rifle over the gentle ridge and levered a shell into the chamber. Jessica crawled up near him.

Aiming at the horse, Ki fired as the nearest rider came within range. The horse seemed to jerk, and Ki fired again. The animal crumpled, throwing the rider, and Jessie chuckled.

Ki fired too quickly at the second man. He turned away, putting spurs to his mount. Ki fired twice more and could not tell if he had hit. The horse and rider were soon out of range. The thrown man stayed down, perhaps playing possum. He would have been helpless on foot since his rifle was on the downed horse several yards away.

"That should slow them up," Ki said, edging back. The others would be cautious about approaching the ridge, and might circle it. Either way would take time. And if the downed man was alive, he would have to ride double with one of the others.

As evening approached they halted on a higher rise and used the binoculars, scanning the plains behind them. Nothing moved that they could see.

"We've lost them," Jessie said.

"Unless they've guessed where we're heading. . . ."

They came to Hanover long after midnight. Even the clerk at the hotel was asleep on a cot behind the desk. Ki woke him gently, and he got up yawning and blinking to give them keys.

Dutch Bradshaw was surprised that he had run onto the blond woman and the Chinaman so quickly. He yelled at his men to get after them, "Spread out—dammit, spread out—!"

But the pursued were well mounted and they did not gain. The country was too hilly for an easy chase, and several of the men dropped far behind. But the hills flowed into the prairie not far ahead, Dutch knew. He ought to be able to run them down then.

They rode all night, mostly walking the horses, and in the morning they were in sight of the two. But despite his urging, they could not run the fugitives to earth. His men straggled, too, some mounted on lesser animals that could not keep up. By early afternoon only Dutch and another man, Hank Betts, were in the lead.

When the first two shots came from the ridge, Hank's horse fell, throwing him heavily. The animal was dead with two bullets in the heart. The rifleman was very accurate.

Dutch yelled, "Stay down!" He turned his horse as more shots came—and he was lucky. Only one shot furrowed his mount's rump. Well out of range he halted and got down as the others came up.

"What happened to Hank?"

"I don't think he was hit. He's lying doggo. They killed his horse." Dutch studied the distant ridge. How long would the two stay there? Probably not long; they would expect him to circle around. . . . He looked at the sky. Another hour until dark.

The two were probably pointing toward Hanover, where the fort was. And they weren't far from it now. He doubted if he and the others could get between them and the town now. Someone would have to carry Hank. . . .

He let the men rest, and when it was dark he rode to find Hank trudging toward him. "The sombitch shoots too good," he said. "Two in the heart from a good distance. I sure am lucky he didn't aim at me."

They made camp where they were, and the men discussed the situation. None of them were for going on. None wanted to face the rifleman, whoever he was. They weren't being paid to get killed. Nothing Dutch could say changed their minds.

In the morning they retreated, with Hank up behind one man. Dutch watched them go, annoyed that he had chosen poorly. He would have something to say to Aaron about them when he returned.

He rode on to the town. Hanover was half asleep when he rode in and got down in front of the first saloon. He gulped a beer and asked the bartender if he had seen a woman and a Chinaman in town. The bartender said he had not seen a Chinaman since he had left Frisco.

Dutch received somewhat the same answer in the next three saloons. He sat at a corner table with a glass of beer before him and wondered if the two had gone to the fort. Maybe they didn't stay in town at all.

Neither of the two would know him by sight, but if he asked too many questions that fact might get back to them. What should he do? He sipped the beer and thought about it. He was probably closer to them here—and luck might still put one of them in his sights. Don't discount luck. . . .
He decided to stay for a few days. If he gave up too easily,

as the other men had done, Aaron would ask difficult questions when he got back.

Jessica wanted two things, a hot bath and a real bed with sheets and a pillow. She soaked in an iron tub, crawled between the sheets, and slept the clock round.

When she woke it was evening again, and she was ravenous. She dressed in a traveling suit with a skirt, put her hair up, and went downstairs to the dining room, where she met Paul Nicholson.

He was surprised to see her. "You're back!"

"Of course."

"I was worried sick! You two skedaddled before the sun was up! You left me behind!"

She put her hand on his arm. "Don't be angry. We had a job to do. Are you going to join me for dinner?"

He nodded. "What kind of a job?"

She led him into the dining room. "Don't ask questions."

"That's *my* job. I'm a reporter, you know."

They sat at a table, and a waiter came and lit the candle between them. When he had gone she said, "I know very well. That's why I say don't ask questions. Now, let's talk about something else."

"You don't have a gun on your hip tonight."

She smiled. "It's in my bag." She lifted it to show him.

"Do you always carry it?"

"Certainly. Why did you decide to become a reporter?"

"My father owned a small-town newspaper, and I worked on it as a boy. Printer's ink got into my blood, I guess. In school I studied journalism and went to Chicago and got a job on the *Star*."

"Are you married?"

"Of course not! No one wants to marry a roving reporter. I haven't had a settled address since I left school."

She looked at him, head on one side. Neither had she a settled address. They were two rolling stones. . . . The waiter came again, and they ordered food, steaks and coffee. He began to talk about various cases he had worked on, and she listened, watching his face. He stirred something within her . . . and she knew he felt the same.

She saw Ki come to the door of the dining room. He looked at her, smiled, and left immediately.

When they finished dinner, Paul lit a thin cigar as they sipped coffee. He had been in Europe the year before, he said, doing pieces on European capitals. His paper was attempting to show its sophistication. Now he was in the West, hoping to discover or uncover something about Aaron Madison, the mystery man.

Jessie offered him nothing in that vein. Perhaps when it was all over . . .

They lingered over coffee; Hanover offered nothing in the way of entertainment save the saloon singers and players, but no respectable woman entered saloons.

They left the dining room, and he put out his hand as they came to the stairs. She took it and they went up slowly; the touch sent a warmth up her arm . . .

"I missed you," he said on the landing, squeezing her hand.

She smiled and leaned against him slightly. In the hall he led her to his room, unlocked the door, and pulled her inside. Turning, he took her into his arms, pushing the door closed.

No words passed between them. He kissed her and she responded eagerly, sighing as she heard him slide the bolt closed, locking them in. She could feel his heart beating quickly against her chest, and his hands slid up and down her back. . . .

★

# Chapter 9

Paul scooped her up and carried her to the bed. He put her down and began to unfasten her clothing—till she picked his hands away and did it herself. He tossed his coat to a chair, pulled off his shirt, and pushed down his pants. But she was naked before him.

Sliding her arms about him, she kissed him passionately, feeling the heavy erection pulsing against her thigh. He swept the blanket back and lowered her to the sheet, then bent and kissed her navel as she squirmed. Her arms pulled at him, and he moved to her breasts, teasing one nipple with his tongue as she moaned and writhed her hips sinuously.

She grabbed at him, and he slid onto the bed, over her thigh, and her hand found his member, guiding it. She moaned again softly as he pushed into her deeply. Her inner muscles tightened and squeezed. . . .

Rotating her hips provocatively, she began a maddening

rhythm that seemed to beat inside his skull. She held him with arms and legs, and as they rolled onto their sides, the rhythm remained constant—he pounded into her and she drew his working body even closer, his breath beginning to come in pants. . . .

Her head moved from side to side on the bed—the pillow had long since fallen to the floor—her insides became tight and rigid, her back arched—and she felt him climax.

She strained for one more moment, then a cry burst from her lips as the orgasm twisted her, making her shudder.

The delicious sexual convulsions subsided slowly as she sighed and nipped one of his earlobes. Playfully they stroked and kissed each other tenderly. Paul rolled onto his back, and her fingers sought his shrinking member, caressing it as he got his breath back. He slid one arm under her and pulled her close to kiss her cheek.

"That was lovely dessert, after dinner. . ."

She squeezed him. "I thought so, too."

"Good enough for another helping?"

"I wouldn't miss it for the world." She sighed contentedly as he moved atop her again.

Jessie and Ki reported to Colonel Harrison the next morning. He gave them coffee in his office and listened as Ki told about their escape from Madison.

"We have to get that man into a federal court," Harrison said. "And I don't see any other way than to use force. It's outrageous the way he's set himself up as a petty king!"

Jessie said, "But we're positive there's an informer here at the fort. He will certainly send news of any operation to Madison."

The colonel sighed deeply. "I suppose you're right. But it rankles! Dammit, it rankles!"

Ki asked, "Your investigation, sir . . . has it turned up anything?"

"No. We've checked out every man, over and over again. No one who has access to secret information is under suspicion. I think the leak must come from Washington, D.C. Those people are a long way from here and probably careless with facts."

Jessie glanced at Ki, but did not argue with the colonel.

Harrison said, "I've just received word that a special commission, composed of high officers and senators, is coming here for a tour of inspection—to add to my other problems."

"What does that mean?"

"It means that I'll have to set up a war game for them, a series of maneuvers. Some of those senators like to play soldier, you know."

Jessie smiled. "You'll have to put on a show for them. . . ."

"Yes. That's what it amounts to, a show." He smiled wanly. "I'll arrange for you two to view it if you like."

"We would like," Jessie said quickly. Ki nodded.


Rinaldo Doren was a man who kept his eyes and ears open. He was an opportunist, a man who lived by his wits. For a long time he had been staying near the Rio Grande. It had been profitable trading in horses back and forth across the river, evading the law rather easily—until the new Mexican commandante proved to be rather more energetic than usual, forcing illegal trade to move out of his area.

Doren had come north, looking for a chance to line his pockets. When he saw the Northstar operation in the Alamos hills, he stopped to study it.

Northstar employed perhaps a hundred men to mine gold in its three veins. From all Doren could learn the ore

59

was very high-grade... very rich. Every few weeks—there was no fixed schedule—wagons hauled ore to the railroad siding ten miles away.

The wagons were guarded, of course, by mounted men with rifles, but they were very slow, being heavily loaded. Gold was heavy as hell; the wagons made deep ruts in the well-traveled road.

Doren watched the operation over several weeks, and evolved a plan. When he had it sketched out, he rode to see Aaron Madison. They had done business before.

He rode up the long hill and was admitted when he sent his name to Madison. He met the big man in his office and received a cigar.

"Where you been, Rinaldo?"

"Down on the border, stealing horses."

Madison laughed. "I don't need any horses."

"I don't have any to sell. I come about gold."

Madison blinked. "Gold?"

Rinaldo told him about the Northstar operation. "Ever' few weeks they sends a shipment of ore to the refinery. It goes by railroad."

"What's a shipment amount to?"

"They vary. Sometimes they send three wagons, sometimes seven. I guess it depends on how much ore they mine. But a wagon holds a lot, couple thousand dollars anyway. Maybe more."

"What's your plan?"

"I figger with five'r six men I can ambush that wagon train, take the wagons to Holton—that's about fifty miles west—put 'em on a train to Denver to the refinery there."

"You can't figure your ass, Rinaldo! You going to put gold ore on a train right after gold ore has been held up and men killed? You'll be in jail the next goddam day."

Rinaldo's lower lip came out. "How would you do it, then?"

"Bring the ore here and store it for a while."

"But I need the damn money! If I bring the ore here, will you advance me money?"

Madison's lip curled. "You want me to furnish men so's you can raid the wagon train—then you want me to store the ore so we can sell it later. And on top of that you want me to advance you money?"

"Dammit, Aaron! We're partners, ain't we?"

"Not the way I see it."

"But I brought you the plan! I went and figgered out how to take the ore—"

"You didn't figger far enough." Madison fished in a box and drew out a cigar, looked at it critically, and rolled it in his thick fingers. "Tell you what I'll do, Rinaldo. I'll put you on the payroll for a couple weeks . . . say fifty dollars' worth. You go bring that ore here, and I'll give you a bonus, maybe another fifty."

Doren's face flushed, then turned pale. "Dammit, Aaron! You throwin' me a goddam bone!"

Madison shrugged. "Tell you the truth, Rinaldo, I don't want that damn ore that bad. Sounds t'me like trouble. I'll have money tied up in it for maybe a year. Then I got to haul it somewheres and get rid of it. . . ." He shook his head. "It don't listen all that good. You take the hundred while you can get it. Before I change my mind."

"You got five-six men I can take?"

"Of course. No trouble about that."

Doren was deflated, his shoulders bowed. "That's a hard deal, Aaron. I'm down from thousands to a measly hundred dollars. . . ."

"I've got second thoughts myself, Rinaldo." He sighed. "But I said I'd do it." He opened a drawer and took out a lacquered box. Opening it he counted out fifty dollars and tossed the money on the desk. "When you want the men?"

Doren picked up the money. "In a couple days." He rose and went to the door. "You gonna put me up in the bunkhouse?"

"Certainly."

"Do I hafta pay for it?"

Madison's voice turned oily. "Of course not, Rinaldo. We're old friends." He waved his hand as the other went out and closed the door.

Doren counted the money in the hallway, then folded the bills and shoved them into his pocket. He had told Aaron everything he knew about Northstar—except one thing. He had discovered that Northstar sold all its gold ore to one firm, and that the firm was a middleman set up by the government in secret. It meant that if the ore was robbed, the government would send in investigators . . . who were likely to be far more tenacious than an ordinary sheriff.

What Aaron didn't know . . . Doren smiled to himself. If something happened now, Aaron would be responsible alone. He himself would be long gone. He would not stay around one minute after the ore was delivered to Aaron.

Let greedy Aaron Madison face the music by himself. Maybe he could buy off the government.

# Chapter 10

Colonel Harrison assigned young Lieutenant McKay to escort Jessica and Ki to the maneuvers. McKay was the same officer who had escorted them to the fort from Hanover.

McKay was slim and natty; he was smooth shaven with a long tanned face and very serious eyes. He clicked his heels as he saluted them at the hotel. "I've been assigned to you, sir and ma'am."

"When do the maneuvers begin?" Jessica asked.

"They have already begun, ma'am, but in another sector. I am instructed to guide you to a particular spot where you can see infantry maneuvers."

"I see."

"And I have several pairs of binoculars for you to use . . . as well as food and drink, ma'am."

"Well, the colonel has thought of everything. . . ."

Ki said, "I suspect the colonel has thought of this young man . . . and he has provided the extras."

Lieutenant McKay grinned. "Very astute, sir."

McKay had brought along an army ambulance for them to ride in, and had an escort of six men. He also provided white dusters for them to don against dust. He was a very thoughtful young man, Jessie said.

They took the road to the fort but turned off before they reached it and followed a two-track road that wound in and out and finally circled to a hilltop. It was the tallest hill in the vicinity, quite bare except for grass on the rounded top, and provided an excellent view of the countryside. Far off to the right they could make out the water tower and the tallest rooftops at the fort. The flag seemed to hang in midair, unsupported by anything; the pole could not be seen.

Lieutenant McKay had a map which he spread out for them. His finger pointed out a valley between ground rises. "The troops will come up this valley." He pulled out a watch and studied it. "In about a half hour—if they are on schedule. They will disperse over these three small hills." He turned, smiling. "You should get a good look at them."

"What about an enemy force?" Ki asked.

"Yes, they are the Blue forces. The Red forces will come from this direction. . . ." McKay's finger delineated a line. "How they will maneuver is up to the commanding officer. I expect we will see what position he will take."

Jessica studied the terrain with a pair of the army glasses. She noticed movement off to the right and focused on it. A column of horsemen and limbers wheeled onto a flat area and halted. She watched them scurry like ants and realized it was an artillery battery. Four guns lined up, pointing in their direction, and men hurried, loading the guns and swinging them around.

She pointed them out to Ki, who also focused his glasses on them. "Twelve pounders," he said. He turned to McKay. "Are they using real ammunition?"

The lieutenant peered at the distant battery. "Only if they are shooting at prearranged targets—out of the range of troops."

As he spoke one of the cannons fired. It took a moment for the sound to reach them. They saw the spurt of smoke, and Jessie, staring through the binocs, saw the gun recoil. The roundshot smashed into a clump of trees far to their left.

"That was a real cannonball," she said.

"Yes. They're firing for effect, well away from the troops."

The second, third, and fourth gun fired, and all the shots were in the same area.

McKay, with his glasses, was peering at the distant valley. "The skirmishers are appearing now. They will come ahead of the main body. . . ."

"Yes, I see them," Jessie said. She swung around as the cannon fired again. Ki gasped suddenly as the roundshot whistled by overhead.

McKay yelled and trained his glasses on the battery. "What the hell—" A second cannon fired, and the roundshot smashed into the hill just below them.

Ki grabbed Jessie and ran for the far side of the hill, where the escort was suddenly galvanized. McKay shouted for them to get down the hill as a third roundshot pounded the hilltop only a dozen yards away!

Two more shots hit the hilltop, plowing up dirt and howling off into space, smashing trees far down the hill.

The driver had turned the ambulance, and they piled into it as it rattled away. McKay scrambled onto his horse and followed as more shots pounded the hilltop. Jessie looked back. Dust was rising from the hill where they had stood only moments ago.

In a few minutes they had left the hill behind, and McKay stopped the ambulance. "Are you all right?"

"Yes . . . What happened?"

"Someone is going to face a summary court," McKay said grimly. "The colonel gave strict orders . . ." He took a long breath. "Thank God you're all right. I'd better take you back to the fort."

McKay took them to the officer's club, then reported to Colonel Harrison. When Harrison came into the club, he was pale. He took Jessie's hands. "That must have been a terrible ordeal for you. I am so sorry—I don't know how such a thing could happen. I have men investigating it this moment. The captain of that battery will be here soon. . . ."

Ki said, "Lieutenant McKay got everyone off the hill in seconds, Colonel."

"Yes, he's a very good man. I'm going to leave you in his charge—I've got to get back to the brass and the senators. I'm sure you understand. . . ."

Jessie said, "We'll be very interested in what the battery commander has to say."

"I'll see that McKay gives you the particulars."

They had lunch in the club with Lieutenant McKay fussing over them like a mother hen. He seemed to take it personally that a battery had fired on them.

"It's outrageous," he told them. "We had a special officers' meeting, and the colonel pointed out that particular hill as being an observation post not to be fired on at any time. The battery commander who disregarded those orders is in line to be cashiered."

They returned to the hotel in Hanover, and as they finished supper the lieutenant showed up. They went upstairs to

Ki's room, and he informed them of the meeting Colonel Harrison had had with the battery commander, Captain Deets.

"Deets had a signed order in writing, directing him to fire on the hill," McKay said grimly.

"How could that happen!?"

"Nobody knows at this moment. All the clerks are being questioned. The order was purportedly signed by the colonel, but of course he did not. The order was sent to Captain Deets as his battery was getting ready to fire. If you remember, several shots were fired before the first ones were directed at the hill."

"Yes." Jessie nodded.

Ki asked, "Is it possible some clerk made out the order and forged the colonel's name?"

"Yes, sir. That's what is being determined now. It seems to be the only possible explanation."

After the lieutenant had gone, Jessie said, "Is it one more attempt on our lives?"

"I think so."

"Wouldn't it have to be arranged in a hurry?"

Ki shrugged. "Unless the colonel had planned to ask us to attend and told several people well in advance." He looked at Jessie. "You don't suppose the colonel is behind —no, that's not possible."

She stared at him. "You're right. It's not possible."

"Yes, the person who *is* behind it is someone with a motive. Someone who wants to get rid of us because of what we might do to him."

"Aaron Madison."

Ki smiled. "If the shoe fits . . ."

"The shoe fits Mr. Madison. His long arm extends into the fort. We don't know how many are on his payroll, but probably at least two."

"I agree. At least two. The man who forged the order is likely to be an officer. But the order was delivered by an orderly—I'm guessing, of course. Which does us no good."

"I think we're dealing with a very clever man—the informant, I mean. He has been able to cover his tracks extremely well so far. The colonel's investigation didn't turn him up."


Aaron Madison sent him five men and a tall, lean man named Howie. Howie was slow-talking and moved like a cat. Rinaldo Doren was edgy about him at first glance.

But Howie was pleasant enough. "What's your plan about this here gold train, Rinaldo?"

"I been over the wagon train route, and there's one good spot for an ambush, right where the road crosses a dry wash."

"All right. Let's go look at 'er. When's the next wagons due?"

"They don't have no schedule. It's just when they got a load. We'll have to camp out and wait for 'em."

"Aaron didn't say nothing about that. . . ."

Rinaldo grinned. "Guess he didn't know it."

"Shit. We'll have to take us a mule with fixin's. It could be a week, huh?"

"It could be," Rinaldo agreed.

Howie swore and went to get airtights, blankets, and a couple of tents packed on a mule. It took an hour. The rest of them filled warbags, tied on slickers, and then set out with Rinaldo in the lead.

In two days they arrived at the wagon road and looked at the ruts. None was fresh, all were well dusted over. "There ain't been a wagon here for days," Rinaldo said. "We could be in luck."

He led them to the dry wash, and Howie looked the spot over approvingly. "Good place to hit 'em."

The winter storm water had carved out a ten to twelve foot draw through a sandy hill, and the wagon road had to go through it, or over the hill. A wagon full of gold ore was too heavy to go over the hill. Obviously none ever had.

Howie placed the men to look down on the road. They would have a terrible advantage over the guards.

And so it proved. They had to wait only a day for the wagon train to appear. Five wagons drawn by black mules came slowly toward them, accompanied by half a dozen mounted men with rifles across their thighs.

When they got close, Howie gave the signal and the Winchesters mowed the mounted men down like ripe grain. They were all gone in the first ripping volley.

The drivers rolled off the seats and cowered under the wagons until Howie's men pulled them out. "Git back up on them seats."

The men stripped the bodies of revolvers and money, then dragged them along the wash to a place under the steep bank. With pounding boots, they caved in the banks on the dead men.

It took five days to drive the wagons to a ford and cross the Red into Madison's territory. Howie sent a man to report to Aaron, and the wagons went on, past the town of Madison, where Rinaldo left them.

He collected his fifty dollars and headed east. He'd had all he wanted of Aaron Madison.

# Chapter 11

Colonel Harrison at Fort Gillespie received a flurry of telegrams from the War Department in Washington concerning the gold ore holdup and murders at the Northstar Mines. The secretary was outraged that six men had been killed.

He noted correctly that the Northstar massacre was exactly the same kind of operation and result as the train holdup and murders.

"The Big Brass says it's Aaron Madison's trademark—and for once I agree," Harrison said to Jessica and Ki in his office. "That's the way he kills."

"He leaves no witnesses."

"Yes. I'm ordered to send men to guard the mines—now that the barn has been looted. It should have been done long before. A troop moved out this morning early. . . ." Harrison rose and paced the office. "It's supposed to be a secret that those mines are practically owned by the government. I'm also ordered to bring the killers to justice. The War Department thinks I'm a goddamned policeman!"

"They have faith in you," Jessie said.

"Well, of course they don't know about *you*. I suppose they think *I* found that stupid train all by myself—so now I can work miracles."

Jessie laughed. "And so you want us to go look at the site?"

"I certainly do. Maybe I can work another miracle."

They chuckled and Ki said, "Well, the ore train is missing. Maybe we can find it."

"The report says it was taken south, across the Red River."

Jessie sighed. "And Aaron Madison will say he never heard of it . . . knows nothing about it."

"That's probably right." Harrison gave them all the reports he had, and a map. The manager at the mines was Luke Sanford. "He's a good man, but they tell me he's a bit stubborn. As I said, I've already sent a troop of cavalry to augment his civilian guards. So the empty barn door is well locked."

Jessie folded the map. "We'll leave in the morning."

Old campaigners, they took only necessities and set out at dawn. It was a three-day journey along a seldom-traveled road that was not marked. The mines were west and south of the fort, on the edge of an area of badlands.

They arrived in the middle of the day to find the mine settlement very primitive. Off to the left, on a level, treeless plain were the tents of the cavalry troop. The mine offices were in a group of weatherbeaten shacks with living quarters attached. The shacks of the miners were scattered about in twos and threes, with rows of privies near them.

The mess hall was a large building with a kitchen behind it and several ovens by the back door. The mines themselves were in the hills about the little settlement, with narrow-gauge tracks running from each to a loading ramp by the road, where half a dozen empty wagons waited. Behind the ramp were corrals holding horses and mules.

As Jessica and Ki rode up, men were coming from the mines to congregate about the front of the mess hall. They dismounted in front of the building with a sign that said: NORTHSTAR MINING, and then went inside.

The shack had a wood floor, plain wood-siding walls, and smelled of tobacco and coal oil. There was a large black stove in the center of the room with a stovepipe extending through the roof. Three men were seated at desks; they all looked up, staring at Jessica.

A tall man with unruly hair, steel-rimmed glasses, and a drooping black mustache, rose and came round the desk. "You must be from Colonel Harrison—I'm Luke Sanford." He held out his hand.

Jessie introduced them and Sanford put his hat on and they went outside. "If you're hungry, we can eat something. . . ."

"We'd rather see the place where the ore train was robbed."

"I'll get my horse," Sanford said, nodding.

It was about six miles away. In the several years the mines had been operating, the wagons had made deep ruts which a child could have followed in pitch blackness.

At the ambush spot the road crossed a dry wash, following it for a short distance as the wash divided a sand hill.

Sanford said, "When it rains in winter we have to hold up the shipments because this wash is a hard-flowing river. One day we'll have to build a bridge—if the mines hold out."

"It would be easy to do," Jessie remarked.

72

"Yes, we have plans for it, but so far the government hasn't wanted to spend the money."

Ki climbed one of the slopes to look down on the wash. There were plenty of places where men could lie in wait and not be seen until they started shooting. He picked up half a dozen brass cases to take back for comparison. When he was about to climb down, he saw something catch a bit of light, glinting in the low brush. He picked it out and found a silver concho. It had a strand of thread still clinging to the hooks on the back where it had been sewn. It had probably been on someone's belt and the threads had worn thin and the concho had pulled off, possibly when the wearer had moved through the brittle brush.

Ki slipped it into his pocket. If they found a man with a concho missing from his belt . . .

Jessie and Sanford were talking as he joined them. Jessie asked, "Have you followed the stolen wagons?"

"Yes. Until they crossed the river into Madison's territory."

"Isn't that evidence enough?"

"What . . . to go down there with cavalry? We can't prove that Madison knew anything about the robbery and murders. He would deny it, of course, and we'd never find the wagons. The ore is probably in a secret place by now, and maybe the wagons are destroyed. . . . We wouldn't find anything."

When they were alone, Ki said to her, "They're willing to write off the five wagonloads, apparently. Everyone seems scared to death of Aaron Madison."

"It's disgusting. But it's also a big problem."

"Madison has to be brought to justice . . . one way or another. It may take a couple of regiments to root him out, if someone high enough up the ladder will give the order."

He showed her the silver concho, and she turned it over

73

and over in her fingers. Ki said, "It's probably made from a Mexican peso or two. . . ."

"It's very pretty. It came off a belt you think?"

"Probably. The owner may not even know it's missing. If we find someone with a belt and one concho missing, we'll know he was at the ambush."

Jessie handed it back. "That's a long, long chance."

They returned to the group of shacks at the mines, deciding to stay overnight before heading back to the fort. Sanford assigned them two cubicles, and they put their warbags and blanket rolls in them, and after supper Ki was approached by one of the men from the office.

It was dark when the man came to the door. Ki invited him inside and closed the door. A single candle lighted the tiny room, and the man spoke softly.

"My name is Emory Tolliver. I've been working with Luke here for a couple of years."

Ki offered the other a long cigar, and Tolliver accepted it with thanks but did not light it. "Luke is a good man, but he's stubborn."

"How so?" Ki asked.

"Well, I've been pressing him for better security for our wagons—and until the robbery-murders he has refused to ask for military guards, saying we didn't need them."

"He's changed his mind now."

"Yes, of course." Tolliver moved to the door. "I want to say that all gold refineries should be notified. That ore is just ore until it's refined. I doubt very much if Madison owns a refinery."

"I'll see that it's done," Ki promised.

They started back in the morning, and the return trip was uneventful. Even the weather cooperated.

When he saw them in the hotel, Paul Nicholson was agitated. "How do you two disappear into thin air!? One

74

moment you're here and the next you're gone for a week!"

Ki laughed. "We have a magic lantern. . . ." He waved and went up to his room.

"We had a chore to do," Jessie said. "There was no time to explain."

"Is there a story in it? Can you explain now?"

She shook her head. Colonel Harrison had told them the incident at the mine was not to be given out to the press. The government did not want to attract attention to the mines.

He asked, "When can you tell me?"

"I don't know. It's not my place to tell you."

He sighed. "You're a difficult woman. . . ."

She patted his cheek. "You mustn't ask difficult questions."

"Then I'll ask a simple one. Will you have dinner with me?"

She smiled. "Of course. With one provision—"

"What's that?"

"Let me have a bath first."

It took a while for boys to run upstairs with hot water and fill a copper tub, but in an hour Jessica came back downstairs in a pale gray traveling suit with a white ruffle at the throat. She met Paul in the dining room, and it was obvious he was surprised and delighted by her appearance. Gone was the gun-toting Amazon, and in her place was a beautiful, willowy woman who drew all eyes as she glided toward him, extending her hands.

She could not talk about her activities, so he related incidents of the many events he had covered . . . and the evening passed comfortably.

After dinner they strolled upstairs and down the hall into his room. With a single candle burning, they undressed and slipped into bed as if they had been doing that very thing for ages.

In the morning Ki inquired about Mexican craftsmen in silver. Were there any such working in the town? A saloonkeeper sent him to see Juan deLara, who lived and had a workshop on the edge of town. DeLara was well known in the area.

The craftsman turned out to be a middle-aged man, dark and barrel-shaped, with white teeth and excellent English. He was a tinker and jack-of-all-trades, he explained, as well as a silversmith.

He looked at the concho, turning it over and over in his hands. He examined it with a magnifying glass and pointed out a tiny mark on the back.

"This is the maker's signature, señor."

"It's two letters."

"Yes. Every silversmith puts his mark on his work."

Ki peered at the mark through the glass. It was a tiny CG that had been stamped into the metal. Someone's initials. All he had to do was find someone, a silversmith, with the initials CG.

"A needle in a haystack," he told Jessie. "How many silversmiths are there in this part of the country? And when we find CG, will he know who owns the belt with the rest of the conchos?"

They reported to Colonel Harrison. Ki gave the brass cases to the lieutenant, who compared them with the others. They matched. "The same rifle was at all three places."

"It shows conspiracy," Harrison said.

"But it tells us only that the *rifle* was at all three places," Jessie said. "It could have been used by three different men."

Colonel Harrison shook his head. "Not likely. Men don't lend rifles indiscriminately. When a rifle is nicely zeroed-in, a man doesn't want someone else changing the sights. I think if we find a man with that rifle, he was there—and a jury will think so, too."

★

# Chapter 12

They sat in Jessie's room at the hotel. Ki said, "Aaron Madison is behind all these murders and robberies. He pays men to do his dirty work so he can say his hands are clean. He probably has a half dozen men to swear to his whereabouts every hour of his life."

"What're you getting at?" Jessie asked.

"We've got a pile of evidence, but none of it points directly to Madison and no one else. He could squirm out from under any of it."

"According to Colonel Harrison that's the problem the government has faced for years."

"I propose we change it."

She made a face. "How?"

Ha paused a moment. "I think I ought to go down there and get into his house."

"No!" Jessica stared at him. "If they find you, they'll kill you!"

"Not necessarily. Not until they find out what I know."

"*Then* they'll kill you!"

Ki chuckled. "I will do everything I can to keep them from it." He gazed at her. "Can you think of another way to get real evidence against him?"

"No . . . I suppose not. But I don't like it."

"I doubt if they expect such a thing. Their security is probably all designed to keep a force of men out. One man, slipping in like a shadow, may well be undetected."

Jessie sighed deeply. "And I suppose you want to go in alone?"

"Yes. The chances are better. Colonel Harrison has information about his office and quarters. It's in a kind of fort on a hill. I'll go over the wall at night."

"All right . . . I'll go along as far as the wall."


Ki dressed in black, shirt, pants, and boots. He wore a shoulder holster, a derringer strapped to his left ankle, a knife at the back of his neck, and a round tin of matches in his pocket. He wore no hat.

They rode to Madison as before, halting far outside the town. The hill, according to the Colonel's information, was west of the town several miles. They could see it from a distance; it looked like a knob poking up from the desert floor.

When they rode closer at night, there were lights on the wall here and there. They got down and went closer on foot to find they were facing the main gate which was closed. Two lanterns hung above it, and they could see figures move on what must be a firestep.

The gate was made of heavy planks, and the wall that enclosed the top of the hill was made of logs, like an old Indian fort. The ground around the fort had been cleared of

79

high brush and trees, and close to the wall all ground cover had been eliminated.

They walked entirely around the fort, and Ki noted half a dozen places where he thought he could easily scale the wall. There were lanterns every fifty yards or so, but the wall did not seem to be heavily guarded. Apparently those inside had little fear that anyone would try to get in.

"They're sitting there like a hen on a nest of eggs, all warm and comfortable," Ki said. "Probably no one has ever challenged this place, so they don't expect it."

"I still don't like you going in there. . . ."

Ki smiled. "Don't jinx me."

"That's the last thing I want to do!" She looked at the sky. "It's too late now. It'll be dawn in a few hours."

They went back to the horses and rode away from the hill. Making camp in a convenient arroyo, they took turns sleeping and passed the day without incident. When night came, they rode close to the hill again, tied the horses in the same spot, and walked around the hill peering at the wall.

Ki picked out a spot. "I'll try to come out this same way—as soon as I can."

"All right. I'll be waiting."

He crept to the dark wall. He had brought along a lariat and now fashioned a loop. Standing at the foot of the wall, he listened, hearing nothing on the firestep above him. Carefully he tossed the loop, and it caught at once on one of the stakes.

He tugged it taut and went up, hand over hand to the top. There was no one near him. He slid over, onto the firestep, and crouched down. There was no one below him. It seemed to be a corral—but it was very dark. He crawled down, hung by his hands, and dropped.

It was a corral. Several horses were startled and he

spoke soothingly, slid over the corral fence, and looked at the big house. It dominated everything on the hill. There were a few lights on, glimmering through curtained windows. The house had two stories; one of the lights was upstairs. Maybe Madison was going to bed. The downstairs light might be in a guard's room.

To his right was a shack with a light inside. It was some distance away, near the main gate. Possibly a guard shack. To his left were several parked wagons and a buggy. He went that way, flitting like a shadow, stopping to listen every few yards.

The big house loomed up. There were a few trees around it to help with the shadows. He crossed to the side of the house and waited, listening. Someone laughed in the guard shack, and he heard it clearly. Sound traveled in the stillness.

He moved along the side of the house, stepping carefully. If he stepped on a branch, it could break with a sound like a pistol shot. The house was stones, cemented together, cold to the touch. There was a door at the back, securely locked, and he swore under his breath. He would have to go in a window.

He tried all the windows at the far side. Two had no glass but were boarded up. Glass was hard to come by. He worked at one of the boarded-up windows and felt it loosening. It was a small window and had been carelessly nailed. He managed to work the nails out with his knife and set the boards aside.

He listened at the open window. Nothing. It was the work of a moment to wriggle through into the house. He found himself in an unused room. It was a big house; there must be several unused rooms. Where was Madison's office?

He opened the door to look at a hallway, very dimly

lighted. The house smelled of cooked food and tobacco. He was about to step into the hall when the front door opened. Ki closed the door to a slit to see a man with a rifle come into the house and speak to someone else.

A second man, who had been sitting around the corner replied and a chair scraped back. He muttered something and went out. The newcomer seated himself in the chair.

The hallway made a T, and the guard was just around the corner, out of sight.

Ki looked at the floor. Hard wood. His boots would make sounds, no matter how softly he walked. But he had to get that guard out of the way. He probably guarded the office.

Sitting down, Ki pulled off his boots. In stocking feet, he slid into the hall and padded to the corner. As he reached it he could hear the man humming to himself. He slid the revolver out of the shoulder holster, took a breath, and stepped around the corner.

The guard was sitting in the tilted-back chair and his eyes widened in astonishment—then Ki struck him hard with the barrel of the pistol. It only took a second. The man slumped and Ki caught the rifle as it slid from the man's lap. He laid it on the floor, replaced the Colt, and lifted the man off the chair and dragged him down the hall to the unused room. He used the man's belt to tie his feet, used the man's wipe to tie his hands behind his back, and left him. He would have a terrible knot on his head. . . .

Madison's office was down the hall to the left. It was a room in the corner of the house and had only two small back windows. Leaving the door open, Ki lighted a lamp and began to examine Madison's desk. All the drawers were locked, but he easily opened them with his knife.

Most of the drawers contained nothing of interest, but in the bottom drawer were three ledgers. Each had a date on the cover, drawn in black ink. He picked the latest and turned the pages.

There were dates and entries, amounts of money, and some cryptic figures which might be a code.

Some of the last entries in the book were familiar—the dates and amounts listed jibed with the payroll robberies.

The book was very heavy. Ki weighed it in his hand. It would be awkward as hell getting over the wall with it. It was large and apparently weighted for some reason. Each page was printed in blue ink, a line of type at the top: AARON MADISON.

Taking out his knife, Ki slit the last dozen pages and rolled them tightly in a sheet of dark blue paper that he found in the front of the book. There was a ball of string in the desk, and he tied the roll tightly. Loose pages were unhandy to carry. He slid the roll into a pocket and went to the door, blowing out the lamp.

As he reached the door, the front door opened and two men stepped inside. One said, "Hey, Jackson, where the hell are you?"

Then he saw Ki . . . and reached for his pistol.

Ki fired a shot just above their heads and ran to the end of the hall as they both ducked flat. There was a closed door there, and a shot followed him as he opened it and slid inside. He was in a bedroom that smelled dusty; there was an unmade bed, a bare mattress and several straight-back chairs. To his left was another door. It led into a kind of storeroom containing boxes and kegs. He locked the door behind him, pushed up a window, and jumped into the night.

As he landed heavily, someone fired a shot, and the bullet rapped into the wood near his head. A man yelled something. Men were coming around the house. Ki ran the other way, losing them in the dark, and came to the wall.

There was little space here between the house and the wall, and it was very dark.

He took out the pages he had rolled up and hurled it over the wall. Maybe Jessie would find it. . . .

When he moved closer and jumped for the firestep, a half dozen men came out of the shadows in a rush, grabbed him, and hauled him down. They hustled him to the house where there were lanterns. Someone said, "It's the China-man!"

Another man said, "Bring him inside." They pushed him into the house and searched him quickly. Quick hands took his pistol, knife, and derringer. A man fingered the *shuriken* he found in Ki's vest.

"What're these?"

"Only decorations," Ki said. The man grunted and left them.

The man he had left in the unused room had been found, and they would have roughed him up, but Aaron Madison appeared. "What's going on?"

There was instant quiet. One of the men told Madison quickly, and the big man stared at Ki.

"Why did you come here?"

"Curiosity."

"Nonsense."

"It's true."

"Curiosity about what?"

"About how you live. I never saw a house this big be-fore."

Madison sniffed. "That isn't a good enough reason." He turned to the others. "Did you search him?"

A man indicated Ki's weapons on the table. "Them's all he had on him."

Madison studied him. "You come here to rob me?"

Ki looked dejected.

A man nudged him hard. "Answer him."

Ki took a breath. "You got more'n me. . . ."

Madison said, "Where was he when you found him?"

"Coming out of your office."

Ki shook his head. "I was about to go *in* the office. Your men were too quick for me."

Madison's eyes slitted. "What did you expect to find?"

"I don't know . . . something to hock maybe . . . ?"

The big man turned away. "Put him in the outside powder room. I'll talk to him later."

They hustled him out a rear door and unlocked a sturdy-looking shed and shoved him inside. He heard a padlock click shut, then they went away.

He was alone in the pitch dark—and Jessie was waiting out there on the other side of the wall.

# Chapter 13

Jessica heard the shots and the shouting—then there was silence. She waited, chewing her lower lip, worrying and helpless to do anything at all but worry.

Had they shot Ki—or captured him?

She waited till dawn approached. Then she had to retreat and ride away, leading Ki's horse. She kept telling herself that no one could take care of himself half as well as Ki. He had come through every scrape—and this one was no different. He was alive and he would find a way to escape them.

She could not allow herself to think differently.

She stopped where they had camped the night before and got down. How could she help Ki? Madison's men had a description of her, she knew. If she went into the town, someone would recognize her, and then she would be in as big trouble as Ki.

But what if she went into town and no one recognized

her? What if she changed her appearance? She might learn what had happened to Ki.

She could put her hair up under her hat so that no one could see she was blond—they would be on the lookout for a blond woman. There was nothing she could do about her clothes—she had no others. But she might slip into town well after dark. . . .

She turned her head, listening. A group of horsemen was approaching. She jumped up the side of the arroyo and peered south. They were still some distance away, but coming directly for her. A half dozen men.

She ran to her horse and spurred up the arroyo, leaving Ki's animal behind. The wash had a sand bottom, and she left no dust cloud. In half a mile she halted and climbed the side of the arroyo again. The horsemen were off to the left—they had not seen her! They seemed to be following a track or a road. She waited, watching them, and they disappeared northward. Were they looking for her?

She and Ki had been seen together often—when they had captured him, wouldn't they look for her? Probably.

*Had* they captured him?

She retraced her steps and waited for dark. Then she put her hair up and rode toward the town of Madison. She got down on the edge of town, tied the bay Horse, and walked along the street, shoulders bowed, trying to look much older than she was.

She walked from one end of the little town to the other and heard nothing. The saloons were noisy but she dared not go in one. A few older men were sitting in chairs along the street, but they paid her no attention.

She had almost returned to the horse when a group of women and children spilled from a shacky house and stood talking while the children whined. Jessie paused in the shadows and listened.

They were talking about food and about washing clothes . . . discussing soaps. Then, as the women began to depart, one mentioned the man they had captured. Her husband had told her he was a Chinaman. They laughed about a Chinaman being caught in Madison.

Jessica sighed and went on. So Ki had been captured!

She retreated to the town of Norris, some forty miles north and west, and there she wired Colonel Harrison, telling him what she could of Ki's plight.

To her surprise she had no reply, but in two days Paul Nicholson showed up. "The colonel asked me to come. He didn't want to use the telegraph without a code. . . ."

They sat in the waiting room of the only hotel in town, huddled in a corner away from others. She said, "He has a message for me?"

"Yes. He told me to tell you he cannot send troops to get Ki out of there. He says it would take five hundred men to do it, and he cannot send any without permission from the War Department. He also said it would be futile to ask."

"Damn!"

"What will they do with him?"

She frowned at him. "You already know how Aaron Madison kills. What is one more to him?"

Nicholson was silent.

She said, "I've got to go back to Madison."

"What! Stick your head in a noose!?"

"I've got to be there if Ki needs me."

"But if they catch you they'll kill you, too!"

She smiled. *"If* they catch me."

"They caught Ki—why can't they catch you?"

"That question has no answer."

"But what can you do?"

She shook her head. "I have no idea. But I've got to be

there." She patted his cheek. "I have to live with myself, you know."

He moaned. "You're being a silly, brainless woman!"

Jessie laughed. "Flattery will get you nowhere." She rose. "Now, I need some sleep." She went toward the stairs.

"I'll help you."

"Help me sleep?"

He smiled. "I'll help you with anything that needs help. One never knows."

"That's true. Come along then. I'll find something for you to do."

Sunup showed Ki a small square room with a barred window. He had slept on a mat on the floor; there was nothing else in the room. The door was opened in the morning, and a man pointed a shotgun at him and showed him to the privy, not far away, then locked him in again.

He could see distant hills through the window, but little else. The window faced away from the house, and there were trees that hid the wall.

The room had obviously been used before as a jail. Various names and epithets were written or scratched on the walls, and someone had cut and pried at the iron bars on the window . . . with no result.

In the middle of the morning the door was suddenly opened again and a plate of food shoved in with a spoon and a small bottle of water.

Nothing else happened all the rest of the day.

Ki sat on the bed mat, leaned against the wall, and wondered why Madison did not question him. Why else were they keeping him alive? He had no illusions about the man. Madison was perfectly capable of putting him against a wall and shooting him. He would call it an execution.

He watched the sun go down, and at dusk the door was opened again and he was ordered out. Three men with shotguns took him into the house and put him into a room, then departed.

In an hour Madison appeared, with two men, and sat across the room from him. The two men took up stations one on either side of the big man, pistols leveled. Ki smiled to himself. They were taking no chances.

He did his best to look as helpless as possible. If they feared him, they would watch him more closely.

Madison said, "Tell me again, why are you here?"

"Money," Ki said. "I hoped to find some money. As I told you, I am a poor man."

"I find that very hard to believe—that you came to rob me."

Ki showed surprise. "Why not? You are the richest man in the territory—everyone says so." His inner surprise was greater . . . apparently Madison hadn't yet noticed that his ledger pages had been cut out! He had put the books back exactly as he had found them—but the desk drawers had been broken open. Maybe Madison assumed that was as far as he'd gotten when he'd been detected. Because of course when he'd been caught, he'd had nothing on his person that belonged to Madison.

Madison asked, "What do you do for a living?"

Ki pretended agitation. "I-I have no profession."

"Where do you come from?"

"What do you mean?"

"Are you Chinese?"

"No. I am half Japanese."

"I see. What is your connection with the blond woman?"

Ki shrugged. "We are merely friends."

90

"She came here to Madison with you. I believe you met the town marshal. . . ."

Ki made a face. "Yes . . . he wanted to put us in jail, and we were merely passing through. We got out of town as fast as we could."

"Why did you come to town?"

"We didn't know the town was there. We came across it—"

Madison got up abruptly. "I believe nothing of what you say. Put him back in the powder room." He went out quickly.

# Chapter 14

Jessica found it necessary to slip away from the hotel long after midnight. Paul Nicholson was determined to go with her, refusing to realize he would be a detriment instead of a help.

She bribed the stable boy to have her horse saddled and ready, and walked the bay from the stable, mounted, and rode out of the town.

She had no plan except to pray that circumstances put her in a position to help Ki. They had agreed he could come back over the wall at a particular spot. She would wait for him there.

When she arrived near Madison's hill fort, it was daylight and she was in time to see, through binoculars, that a buggy and half a dozen riders were leaving the main gate. There were two men in the buggy and she thought one answered Madison's description.

None of them was Ki.

She followed the group to the town, but dared not enter herself.

When night fell, she rode back to the hill and tied the bay horse, then walked cautiously to the spot under the staked wall to wait.

Ki did not appear.

Near sunup she went wearily back to the horse and found a spot several miles away to rest. She would return that night.

Aaron Madison went to meet Senator Francis Yarrow, taking along an escort of six men, led by Howie. Yarrow was part of his grand plan for the future, an important part, and Aaron was worried about him.

Yarrow, he thought, was essentially a weak man, a worrier and too cautious. The plan he envisioned needed men who were bold and definite, not afraid of odds, fighters like himself. He wondered if Yarrow was under his wife's thumb . . . of course, he denied it when the hint was made, but Aaron suspected it. She was the definite one in that family.

And the time was drawing near. Soon it would be winter again—and another year had passed. Aaron sighed deeply. He was forty-seven now, getting on. It was eleven years since he had first envisioned the grand plan and enlisted Yarrow and the other five senators.

But a great deal had been done. Now all that remained was to go forward boldly. Could Yarrow do that?

He was not at all sure.

They had agreed to meet in a little town on the stageline, Hondo. Yarrow would be coming from Louisiana. Aaron hoped he had left his wife behind.

It was a long, dusty trip, and while he swore at the dust it was better than being held up for days when bridges

93

washed out. He had brought along Wilbur Dunning, who was a secretary and valet combined, as well as an excellent cook.

The men set up a tent for him each night, and Wilbur managed a decent supper, served on china plates, and all in all that sort of roughing-it was acceptable.

However, he was glad to see the town appear in the green valley ahead . . . and know he was going to sleep in a bed that night, not on a mat on the ground.

Yarrow was not there when he arrived. Wilbur went to the stage office and brought back a schedule . . . and Aaron sent him to meet each stage from the east. Yarrow came in two days later, protesting that he was battered half to death.

An hour's soaking in a tub improved his disposition, and dinner with Aaron, with a real tablecloth and silver, made him feel less of a savage in a wild land.

He had come alone, knowing, he said, that the journey would be rigorous. Aaron thought he wanted to be considered a hero for his mighty efforts . . . so Aaron flattered him outwardly and despised him inwardly.

Francis Yarrow was a thin, sallow-faced man with deep furrows alongside his nose. He was clean-shaven except for a fuzzy goatee. His eyes were pale and listless and his political enemies called him Mr. Put-It-Off because of his everlasting caution.

However, his wife prodded him to take advantage of his position to become wealthy. So far he had not amassed much of a fortune. He had high hopes that his partnership with Aaron Madison would make him not only rich but powerful.

Over dinner Aaron expressed again his concern that things were moving much too slowly.

"But Aaron, some things should not be rushed."

"I'm not speaking of rush, Francis. I am speaking of normal, regular progress."

"Progress in which direction?"

Aaron concealed his impatience. "For one thing, we need a force of men—call them anything you wish, even policemen, but we need a force to protect us. To protect what is ours."

"An army!? A private army?"

"A state militia, if you prefer. I'm not choosy about names."

"Such a thing, if it became known, would be considered an overt act by the federal government!"

"I'm talking about a secret force. I'm well aware the time is not yet ripe for any disclosure." Aaron leaned forward and lowered his voice. "I already have the core of it, and the plans. But I need a military leader. Ambrose Coyle was a major general in the war . . . would he serve?" Ambrose was one of the five senators.

Yarrow pulled at his goatee. "It would mean he'd have to leave the Senate immediately. I don't know what he'd say."

"Then I'll write him at once."

Yarrow took a long breath. "Aaron, can't all this be done peacefully? Do we need troops?"

Aaron stared at the sallow man. "If we need them and don't have them—we're all through, all of us. Some will call us traitors, you know."

"Traitors!?"

"And I'm sure hanging will be mentioned. You know how people can be inflamed. Yes, we need a force of men. When you return to Washington, you must take Ambrose

95

aside and reason with him. We need an experienced military man and we need him desperately."

"God!" Yarrow said in a hollow voice. "Traitors?"

When they brought Ki his meal in the middle of the day, they let him eat, then they took him out of the little powder house and put him into one of the upper rooms of the big house. Mr. Madison wanted to see him when he got back, they told him.

It was a smallish room that had been recently remodeled; the bars on the two windows were new and had been hammered in with spikes. The floor had no carpet and there was only one chair and one cot. There was wallpaper on three walls, small roses entwined with white leaves. A peephole had been made in the door.

When they opened the door to give him food, he was required to back up to the opposite wall. Sometimes one man delivered his tray alone, but occasionally a second man was with him, with a shotgun.

When the man came alone, Ki asked him why he had been brought into the house, and the man replied that it was easier for them.

"When will Madison be back?"

The man glanced into the hall. "I dunno. Few days, I 'spect."

"What will they do with me?"

The man shrugged and grinned. "They prob'ly gonna shoot you." He went out and slammed the door.

It was all he could get from the man. He only shook his head when Ki spoke to him.

It was time to get out.

He could assume that no one had found the rolled-up pages he had tossed over the wall. Apparently they had fallen into weeds and not been noticed. And Madison had not yet noticed the pages were missing. Perhaps he only made entries at long intervals.

He decided to wait until nightfall. The man with the tray came at different times, often quite late, and the food was always cold when he did. It was no skin off his butt.

Ki stood against the wall when the door opened. The man was alone. He took two steps into the room and laid the tray on the floor. As he looked up, Ki hurled a *shuriken*. It tore his throat out and he collapsed with hardly a groan.

The man lay in a pool of blood that spread out quickly. Ki pulled off the dead man's holster; it held a .44 Colt. He retrieved the throwing star, wiping it clean, and went to the door, the revolver in his hand.

The hall was empty. When he walked to the end of it, he could hear voices downstairs. How long would it be till someone came up to see why the other had not come down?

He hurried to the other end of the hall and found himself in a large bedroom—was this Madison's bedchamber?

There were three windows. He opened one and looked out at a thick pine tree. The ground was a long way down, but the house had only one staircase and he had no idea how many armed men were at the bottom of it.

He climbed out of the window and jumped for the tree.

He slid down partway, then let go and dropped. There was a thick carpet of pine needles under the tree, and it cushioned the fall. He leaned against the tree and looked about. No one made an outcry; no one had seen or heard him.

The log wall was only a few dozen steps away, and he started toward it when he heard voices. Ducking back to the tree, he crouched as a man with a rifle came walking along under the wall. Ki realized he had just spoken to someone on the firestep above him.

Moving slightly, Ki saw the sentry on the wall, the man silhouetted against the lighter sky, staring outward. When the man with the rifle passed, disappearing into the gloom, Ki followed, noting that there was a sentry every fifty yards or so. These men paid no attention to those below them on the ground inside.

He came to the place where he'd climbed over. The rope was gone; evidently someone had noticed and taken it. He slid into the corral, onto the poles, and climbed up easily to the firestep. The wall was probably ten or twelve feet high as an average, he thought. He climbed over the parapet, let himself down slowly, holding by the hands, and dropped.

It was only a few feet and noiseless.

He remained motionless, waiting for an outcry—but none came. He had not been detected.

In a moment he heard a low peculiar-sounding whistle. It was the signal he and Jessica had used many times before, and he answered it instantly, moving silently toward the sound.

In a few moments Jessica came out of the gloom, grinning at him. "I knew you'd get away from them!"

# Chapter 15

In his own hotel room after leaving Francis Yarrow, Aaron stood at a window and thought about their conversation. Each time he met and talked with Yarrow he worried more about the man. Yarrow was senior to the other five senators, but in Aaron's opinion, the weakest.

He was the weak link. When the plan was finally announced to the world, there would be a great outcry—perhaps. And that was the time for certain men to stand fast. Aaron had no faith at all that Yarrow would be anything but a brittle twig. He should never have picked the man in the first place.

But what should he do now?

Was there any chance that Yarrow would cave in and go over to the other side . . . the opposition? Aaron thought of opposition as the other side.

There was a great chance he would do that, wasn't there?

The more he thought about it, chewing and worrying the thought, the more convinced he was. Francis Yarrow knew everything about the plan, and a few words from him in the right places might destroy it utterly.

Aaron's fists clenched. His entire future was in the hands of a weakling! His very life was in the trembling hands of an ass like Yarrow!

He went downstairs and sent a boy for Howie.

A half hour later the tall, lean man rapped on the door, and Madison let him in and locked the door behind him. He motioned Howie away from the door and spoke softly. "Do you know Senator Yarrow by sight?"

"Yes, sir, I do."

"You're absolutely certain?"

"He was pointed out to me in the stage waiting room, and his bags had his name on them."

"All right." Madison regarded the other. "Dutch tells me you're a man who can be depended on."

Howie nodded.

"There's a job that needs doing, and I wonder if I can depend on you to do it."

"Something concernin' Yarrow, sir?"

"Yes. Unfortunately Yarrow has outlived his usefulness. He has become a very great liability. Do you understand me?"

Howie smiled thinly. "Yarrow has got to go, sir."

Madison nodded. "You *do* understand."

"Is he the only one, sir?"

"Yes. The only one. Can I leave this all in your hands?"

Howie nodded. "You don't want it done here in town . . . ?"

"No. It would be better another place." Madison paused. "When it's over, come and see me. I'll have a bonus for you."

Howie seemed about to speak, then said nothing.

Madison smiled. "Five hundred dollars. Is that sufficient?"

Howie smiled back. "D'you know when he's leaving town?"

"Tomorrow, I think. He'll take the stage."

Howie nodded again and went to the door.

Madison said, "Not a word to anyone else."

"Yes, sir." Howie went out, closing the door gently.

He paused on the street and looked at the sky. Five hundred dollars! Very few times in his life before had he been able to scrape together that much . . . in one pile. When he had it, money seemed to flow through his fingers.

But this time it would be different.

He sat in a chair in front of the dry goods store and tilted it back, staring at the front of the hotel. How should he do this? Yarrow would be on the eastbound stage, so why not hold it up and shoot Yarrow in the process? If he robbed everyone, it would seem like an ordinary holdup.

He couldn't think of a better idea.

He ambled across to the stage waiting room and looked at the posted schedules. There was an eastbound stage leaving town the next afternoon. Madison had been right.

In the morning he would ride out along the route and look for a good spot, then wait for the stage. It ought to be a cinch. He smiled, thinking that Dutch had put in a good word for him. He'd buy Dutch a drink when they got back.

He said nothing to the others, had a few beers with them, listened to a few girls singing in the Red Hat Saloon then went to bed.

After breakfast he slipped down to the livery and rode out of town after asking the stable owner about the road north.

He rode east for ten or twelve miles and found a place where the road went up a rather long hill. The six horses would probably go up it at a walk. He made himself comfortable in a rocky niche near the top and waited.

It took forever for the stage to come along. Howie dozed and shook himself awake half a dozen times. He had no watch so he had no idea of the time. The sun told him it was afternoon—and the sounds finally told him the Concord was on its way.

Taking off his hat, he watched the stage come toward him. He put the hat back on and fired a shot with the Winchester. The driver hauled back on the reins, and the guard on the box turned toward him. Howie stood up with his wipe about his lower face. He aimed the rifle. "Don't do it—"

The guard stopped and slowly put the shotgun across his knees. Howie said, "Toss it in the brush."

The guard did as he was told.

"Passengers out," Howie ordered. He watched them climb down, four men. Yarrow was the third to come out.

He ordered them to put their money in a pile on the ground. One man started to take his watch and chain off, but Howie motioned him to stop. He didn't want the watch. It could be evidence against him.

When they finished, he ordered them into the stage again, and when they were settled, he stepped to the door with the Colt and shot Yarrow twice in the chest.

Someone yelled and he saw Yarrow's eyes, huge in the dim light. His body rolled forward and Howie fired another shot over the driver's head. "Get a-moving!"

The coach rolled away, tires gritting on the hard ground. He picked up the pile of money and stuffed it into his pockets and hurried to his horse. It had been a cinch. As he mounted he watched the stagecoach in the distance, and grinned, thinking of those men having to ride with a corpse to the next town. They'd have plenty to talk about.

He rode back to town slowly, arriving at dusk.

Jessie had not brought another horse, so they rode double, putting as much distance as they could between them and the house on the hill. There would be much swearing when they found the body. . . .

He told Jessie about his capture and the subsequent days and how he had tossed rolled-up pages over the wall.

"We've got to go back for them."

She said, "Not yet. It's too dangerous."

"We have to find them before it rains."

"That's weeks away."

He hoped she was right.

They returned to Hanover and sent a message to Colonel Harrison. He sent Lieutenant McKay with an ambulance to bring them to the fort.

Harrison looked very worried. "Washington is jumping up and down and screaming at me. They seem to think I robbed that damned ore train!"

Jessie said, "They have to have someone to blame."

"Yes. I wish they'd blame the robbers. They say I haven't shown any results."

Harrison paced the office, hands clasped behind him. Jessie said, "Have you mentioned Aaron Madison to them?"

He halted and looked at her. "We know there's an informer somewhere—either here on the post or in Washington. But I have no hard evidence to give them. They like to deal in hard facts. If I say that Aaron Madison has an informer here—they'll ask me who he is."

"That's ridiculous!"

"Of course it is. But we're dealing with bureaucrats, my dear. They don't think like ordinary people. It would never occur to them that—If I told them there was an informer in our midst, the informer would hear it and dig himself in deeper."

Ki said, "Are they sending in their own investigators?"

The colonel looked at him. "Very astute. Yes, they are. They will report to me when they arrive."

"Who are they?"

"I have no idea. They may be army or they may be civilian. I'll tell them to investigate the train robbery—*if* they listen to me. So you went into Madison's stronghold! What did you learn?"

Ki told him about the pages he had stolen from Madison's ledger. "They seemed to match the dates and amounts of the several robberies. I cut the pages out with a knife, and they were not missed during the time I was there."

Colonel Harrison smiled. "You're a very slippery young man! I'm glad you're on our side."

"I think I could have gotten away almost any time, but I wanted to talk with Madison again—but they told me he was gone somewhere. I finally decided not to wait."

As they were talking with the colonel, an orderly rapped on the door with a message for Harrison. The colonel took the paper and came back into the room reading it.

"A rather odd bit of news just came over the wire," he said. "A United States senator was killed by a holdup man who was in the act of robbing a stagecoach."

Jessie asked, "Was anyone else harmed?"

"No, apparently not." He frowned at her. "Are you saying it might have been an assassination?"

"Who was the senator?

"Francis Yarrow. Have you heard of him?"

Jessie shook her head. Ki said, "No. Where did the holdup take place?"

"It doesn't say. I expect we'll have more details later. But why should a holdup man shoot a senator? Surely the senator did not challenge him. . . . Such men are not wild kids."

"Yes, it is odd. . . ."

They returned to the hotel in Hanover, and Paul Nicholson was waiting for Jessica. He had learned she was back, he said, and worried about her.

"It's sweet of you," she said, "but I am not a fragile flower."

"Yes, I know that very well. Is that your pistol in your bag?"

"One is," she said, smiling. She showed him a derringer with a flick of her wrist. "The other is here."

"Jesus! You are so quick!"

She touched his nose with a finger. "Remember to always say nice things about me."

He laughed. "I certainly will! Is your friend, Ki, as quick as you?"

"Much quicker." She took his arm. "Come, let's have supper. I'm famished."

# Chapter 16

Two men presented themselves at the gate of Fort Gillespie; their credentials said they were investigators working for the Pindar-Schol Agency, on contract to the War Department.

Colonel Harrison received them in his office after Major Jennings had checked their vouchers and admitted them. One man was Jules Beecher, the other Floyd Kendrick. Beecher was stout and red-faced with small pop-eyes; Kendrick was skinny and sullen-looking. Harrison was not impressed by either.

They had a sketchy idea of the circumstances, probably gleaned from newspapers, and were very interested, they said, in the train robbery. Beecher said he believed it to be the key to the entire affair.

"By all means, go and look into it," the colonel invited. He had decided, in the first few minutes, to get rid of the two of them as quickly as he could. He showed them on a map exactly where the robbery-murders had taken place, and where the train had been recovered.

"Has the money been found?" Kendrick asked.

"Not a penny of it."

The two looked at each other. Beecher said, "Then with your permission, Colonel, we'll go there at once."

"By all means." Harrison showed them out.

When they had gone, he called in Jennings. "If those two show up again, get rid of them. I don't want to see them."

"Yes, sir."

They obtained horses from the Hanover Livery, put them on the next eastbound, and arranged with the conductor to be put off at the dirt-covered siding.

They rode south to the end of the line, where the train had been found, and examined the surrounding terrain. The area had once been a thriving mining district, now played out. The hills about them were pocketed with mineholes, dozens of them; some investigatory scratches and some deep and well-shored mines, a few with narrow tracks still in place.

"This is where the money is," Kendrick said with confidence, rubbing his hands together. "It's exactly the same operation as the Efteland affair. The robbers buried the money and came back a year later to get it, when all the hue and cry had died down."

"We'll have to have a gang of men. . . ."

"We can get them in Kearny."

"Yes . . . let's go."

Beecher had been in the construction business before he became an investigator, and he quickly organized the search. He hired the men, arranged for a mess tent and cooks and for a row of sleeping tents. In two days after the

107

men and material arrived, the area was transformed.

Kendrick had mapped the search area and decided where they would begin, and crews of diggers began the search for the missing army payroll.

Beecher and Kendrick were convinced it had been hidden in one of the old mines.


Aaron Madison raged when he returned to find Ki had escaped. It took him an hour to calm down enough to talk sensibly. One man had been killed, his throat torn out.

"How could that happen? He had no knife!"

"We don't know," Dutch said. "It didn't look as if he did it with his bare hands. . . . "

"Not a shot fired—?"

"No."

Madison waved them out. The man, Ki, must have had a weapon they hadn't found . . . some sort of Oriental trick. Well, no use mewing over spilt milk. . . .

What should he do with the gold ore train? Rinaldo Doren had made it sound so easy. . . . But now he had money tied up in the train and no way of getting it out. The wagons had been stored in an old barn for the time being, and now he was forced to guard them.

It was a very annoying situation—and Rinaldo long gone. He wished he could get his hands around the man's throat.

He needed a refinery—or he needed to sell the lot. The latter seemed the best bet. But who would buy it?

Gold ore was out of his field of experience. He had fifteen or twenty thousand dollars' worth just sitting, costing him money to guard—it was infuriating.

And now that Francis Yarrow was dead, he had to meet with the other five senators as soon as possible. The plan must not be allowed to wither on the vine; if it did not go forward it might well stagnate. He set about composing a letter to be sent to each one. Could each man come to Madison?

The newspapers had been generous with Yarrow, printing an early photograph of him, detailing his life but leaving out his failures. Aaron was disgusted reading them. Francis had been a money-grubbing hack, if the truth were known.

The law had apparently accepted the surface facts, that Yarrow had been shot by a holdup man. There was speculation about the act—why had Yarrow been singled out? The other passengers had all agreed, Yarrow had made no move, said nothing at all—and the robber had shot him.

Several Eastern papers had mentioned assassination, but no proof could be found . . . and the assassin *had* robbed the passengers.

Howie had not handled the situation as well as he might have, Aaron thought, but Howie was not a man with imagination and flair. He was a gunman and had gunned down his prey as he had been ordered.

Aaron sighed. He was surrounded by lesser men. He could admit, though grudgingly to himself, that he needed men like the half Japanese, Ki, who had escaped him. Where could he find men like that?

Several days passed before Ki and Jessica decided to return to the hill fort to look for the rolled-up pages. They had no way of knowing whether or not they had been found and returned to Madison. But the search had to be made.

It was going to be difficult, searching for a tiny object in darkness, close under the wall where sentries would shoot at anything suspicious.

Once more Jessica avoided Paul Nicholson and they rode away from the town late at night. When they arrived near Aaron Madison's hill, the moon was only a thin sliver in the sky with stars aswarm but giving no light.

Leaving the horses, they picked their way through the dark sea of night to an area where Ki thought he had tossed the pages. The wall loomed darkly only yards away, and as they searched the ground, they could easily hear the voices of the guards, chatting, swearing, and grumbling. Grass and weeds had grown up over the once-cleared area, not near enough to conceal a man in daylight but tall enough to hide a small, rolled-up bit of paper.

They were as thorough as possible, quartering the ground, searching every inch, but after several hours their backs were aching and they had found nothing.

When they returned to the horses, Ki mused that they might have searched the wrong area. It was difficult to be positive about the exact spot he'd tossed the pages. It had been dark then, too.

They rode far out, away from the town and made a cold camp, then came back and searched the ground the next night, finding nothing. Was it possible someone lounging on the wall had noticed the small packet and been curious enough to investigate?

After the third fruitless and tiring night, they had to give it up for the time being. They were out of food—they could not go into the nearby town of Madison. And so they retreated. It was discouraging.


Dutch Bradshaw was very annoyed that Howie had been selected over him and been given an assignment that had paid him five hundred dollars! Howie could not help bragging about it and about how easy it had been.

When Dutch went to Aaron to protest, Aaron reminded him that he had been given an assignment he had not yet carried out . . . the elimination of the blond woman and the Oriental.

"Hell, that's impossible for one man alone!"

"Why?"

"Because them two are slippery as fish and damned fast with guns."

"That's why I offered so much," Aaron said. "Does that mean you refuse the assignment?"

"No, sir." Dutch shook his head quickly. "But it's gonna take time just to locate 'em."

"All right." Aaron selected a cigar and took his time cutting off the end. "I've got another project, and you will fill the bill just fine."

"What's that?"

"I want you to go to Corona. You know where it is?"

" 'Bout a hunnerd miles east."

"Yes, that's right. I'm told that the bank there, the Parker Trust, handles large amounts of cash which is sent to Fort Smith each fortnight."

Dutch looked puzzled. "What's a fortnight?"

"Two weeks. I'm also told that the shipment wagon is well guarded. You'll have to go into the bank. Take as many men as you'll need. All right?"

Dutch nodded.

"This conversation is just between us. You will receive a bonus of two hundred dollars more than the others."

Dutch nodded again. "Corona—Parker Trust."

"Exactly."

# Chapter 17

Aaron Madison wrote to Ambrose Coyle, asking him to come to Madison before the others, hinting that Ambrose was the most important of the group.

Ambrose took the bait—at any rate he showed up, arriving on an afternoon stage with several bags and an aide, Merle Loomis, whom he introduced as his secretary.

Wilbur Dunning met the stage and escorted the two up the long hill to the fort house where Aaron greeted them effusively and that evening provided them an excellent meal of roast beef, several vegetables, and brandy.

Ambrose Coyle was a tall, elegant-looking man with white hair and a flowing white beard. His face was pink and relatively unwrinkled despite his near seventy years. He was a graduate of the Military Academy at West Point and had served in the army for eleven years before the war, then entered business and become successful. The army had called him back for the war where he had rapidly risen to general rank, and after the war he had gone into politics.

After dinner the two men retired to a smaller room alone, and Aaron closed the door and brought out a bottle of brandy and glasses.

Coyle asked at once, "How is the plan progressing?"

"Slowly. Cash is always a problem. There are so many mouths to feed."

"Are you asking me for money?"

Aaron stared at the other in surprise. "Of course not! We manage somehow." He forced a smile. "What I am asking you for is your experience. I have no one here who could train and equip a fighting force. Francis and I discussed that very topic before his unfortunate death."

"That *was* curious. Did you investigate it?"

Aaron shrugged. "I? No. I suppose the local sheriff looked into it."

Coyle poured into a glass. "Did you get along with Francis?"

"Of course! We had small disagreements but nothing that would cause enmity. I held Francis in the highest regard. I am sure you know that." Aaron's voice was tinged with surprise.

Coyle sipped the brandy and shrugged. "He could be difficult. How many men can you raise?"

"Possibly two hundred—If I pay them well."

"Those are men from this area?"

"Yes. But I think if we began raising a corps, other men would come to join us."

"Yes, undoubtedly. Especially if we paid them. The pay is essential because we have no great mission to advertise. The plan must remain secret as long as possible."

Aaron nodded. "Exactly. I am collecting cash wherever I can . . . I doubt we will ever have enough. We will run up debts that can be paid off later."

113

"That is your affair. Do not concern me with it."

"All right." Aaron smiled inwardly. This man was certainly definite.

"If we begin equipping and drilling a force, can it be done in secret?

Aaron nodded. "There is an easily guarded valley south of here, far from any settlement. I am sure secrecy can be provided for a year or more. Will it take longer?"

"To train infantry? No. What about officers?"

"I don't know. You must tell me."

"Uniforms?"

"We will buy them, and rifles, too. I have contacts who will supply all we need."

Coyle nearly smiled. "Good." He reached for a cigar and rolled it in his fingers. "Barracks and other buildings?"

"I will send for carpenters. They are part of my cash problem. Will you resign from the Senate?"

Coyle did not answer for a moment. He lit the cigar and puffed, then looked at the glowing end. "I will try to take a leave of absence . . . but the matter deserves more thought."

Aaron did not press him. It was not a satisfactory answer, but he would return to it at a later time.

They retreated to the town of Norris, about forty miles away. There was a telegraph and they reported to Colonel Harrison that they'd had no luck but would not give up.

Harrison replied that he was sending them a letter, in care of the Norris postmaster. It should arrive within the week, addressed to Jessica Starbuck.

They made another four-day round trip to the hill fort and back, searching at night for the pages, and did not find them. They were detected—the sentries must have heard something—they were fired on when they did not answer a challenge. But they easily evaded the fire. Bullets tore up

114

the ground behind them as they slipped away to the waiting horses.

The letter had not arrived when they returned to Norris.

Remembering the concho Ki had found, they made inquiries about a silversmith and were informed that Consuela Garcia had a small shop near the stageline depot. She and her father and brother worked in silver.

"Her initials are CG," Ki said, "the same as the maker's mark on the concho. I'll go see her at once."

"She must be the one," Jessie agreed.

She was. She recognized the concho at once, turned it over, and pointed to her mark. She was a comely young woman, slender and dark, wearing a work apron, with her hair pulled back severely and tied with a red ribbon.

The shop was not large, a tiny front section with glass cases containing silver items, many worked with bits of jade, turquoise, topaz, and other stones. The workshop was behind a curtain where Ki could hear someone at work shaping and grinding.

Ki asked, "Can you tell me who you made this for?"

"Mr. Bradshaw," she said at once. "I made an entire belt for him—this is one of the pieces."

"He is a good customer?"

"Yes. He likes silver—and he gives many presents to señoritas. How did you get this?"

"I found it," Ki said. "The owner is a Mr. Bradshaw? What is his first name?"

"They call him Dutch."

"And he works for Aaron Madison?"

She shrugged. "I do not know."

He thanked her and returned to the hotel where Jessie was waiting. "She made it for a man named Dutch Bradshaw."

"Who works for Madison?"

115

"She said she didn't know that."

"But it's obvious. Where there's smoke, there's fire. This man, Bradshaw, is probably one of Madison's killers."

The colonel's letter arrived the next day, and they read it together in Jessica's room.

Many reports had been sent him, Harrison wrote, about families who were being pushed off their land by armed thugs. There had been killings and houses and barns burned to the ground. People blamed Aaron Madison.

The latest outrages had occurred near Coopersville. Harrison asked them to investigate to see if the charges were true and valid. If they were he would send troops to restore order.

It meant giving up the search for the pages . . . but they had to comply.

Coopersville was some distance south and west of Norris, high and dry on the plains, a crossroads town that had been a trading post in the beginning and now served a few ranchers and sod-busters, and apparently made a dismal living from it.

The town, Ki thought, had a hangdog look, and the first saloon he entered was deserted, the single bartender half asleep behind the bar.

He ordered a drink. "The town doesn't look prosperous."

The bartender, a stout man with sparse black hair combed across his pate, stared at him. "You work for Aaron Madison?"

"I do not," Ki said definitely. "I know the name, that's all."

"That name ain't very pop'lar around here jest now. You passin' through?"

Ki nodded. "Heading for Hanover." He sipped the drink. "What's it all about, this Madison?"

The bartender glanced at the door. "Hell, he grabbin' land. The sonofabitch got half the goddam country now, with his cows on it. But that ain't enough f'him. Hell, no. He got to have it all!"

"How's he getting it?"

"Foreclosin' loans. Pushin' people off'n their land. The land they been a-working for years."

"Can he do that?"

"That's what we askin'. But he got the lawyers on his side. Judges, too. You go to court with Aaron Madison, you goin' to lose ever' time. He tie you up in a nice legal knot and kick your ass out. You wind up with nothing."

Ki nodded. "Why don't the people band together and hire their own lawyer?"

The bartender pointed a blunt finger. "That's jest exactly what they done . . . 'bout a year ago. Madison's toughs run the lawyer off. Shot holes in 'is coat tails. We ain't seed a lawyer since. Can't get one to come here."

"Are you staying?"

"Hell, no. I'm gettin' out, too. Think I'll go back East, maybe to Kansas City."

"And the other people in town . . . ?"

"They gettin' out, too, most of 'em. You mentioned this here town don't look prosperous? Well, we dyin' on the vine. This time next year they goin' be sagebrush rollin' through this here saloon. Coopersville gonna be a memory. Nothin' left—all gone up in smoke and dust. And if there's anything left standin', Madison'll burn it down."

"Has he done this before?"

"Hell, yeh. They was a town over west, Markey. Named after old man Markey who was a gen'ral in the Reb Army. Well, Madison's men, they drove ever'body off and burnt the goddam town to the ground. Nothin' left there now but grass and rattlesnakes and a few cows. And he fixin' to do the same thing here."

Ki reported what he'd heard.

Jessica had heard much the same thing from a storekeeper and a woman who ran a small restaurant. The grocer was positive Madison had destroyed the bridge to the south to keep people from coming into town. Others had been shot at.

They all knew about Markey and feared the treatment.

A few old timers said they would not move, to hell with Madison, but a few at Markey had said that, too. And they were still there, six feet under. "Where we going to go?" they asked. They had come into the country with a wagon and a rifle, but they were too old to do it all again.

"There's no way to fight Madison," they said. "He wants this land for cattle grazing. . . .

"And he gets what he wants."

★

# Chapter 18

Dutch Bradshaw picked three men to go with him to Corona: Hank Betts, Charlie Showdin, and Will Toomis, all hard cases. They had worked for Aaron Madison several years, drawing their pay whether they did anything or not. When a man had no other trade than pistoleer, the steady cash was welcome.

Aaron mentioned this to them now and then.

They all knew that if they made a good haul at Corona, they would get bonuses. Aaron did not have a broad, generous streak, but he was not a penny-pincher, either. He might even send them to Kansas City for a week or two as he had after the train holdup.

It was a long way to Corona, across the plains and a tongue of badlands that held them up for a day. But the town was just beyond, sprawled across a sluggish muddy river that they crossed on a rickety wooden bridge.

They arrived toward evening, with light enough to see

the Parker Trust Bank, the only bank in town. They walked the horses slowly past, looking the town over. It did not seem run-down; new buildings were going up, and it had an air of busyness, even at dusk. Half a dozen saloons were going full blast, and a bevy of painted women yelled at them from upstairs windows. They waved back.

A passerby directed them to a boardinghouse, Mrs. Lott's place. "No smoking in the rooms, gents. That'll be fifty cents a night . . . cash in advance."

They put their horses in the stable, oats were extra, and told Miz Lott they were just passing through and needed to rest up a mite. She gave them supper for twenty-five cents more each.

After supper they sat on the porch for a smoke, then went into town for another look at the bank. It had a big plate-glass window with gold leaf in a crescent; it was the largest building on the street and had offices upstairs, a dentist and a land company.

Dutch indicated the bridge, "That's the only way north. We could head for the badlands . . . what you figger?"

Hank said, "Why not go south?"

"What's south but flat country?"

Charlie pointed. "They's a road runs alongside the river. We could head west."

Will shook his head. "We oughta go over the bridge and into the badlands, like Dutch says. If they's a posse after us, we can sure as hell find a good ambush spot. We got four rifles to kick up a storm."

Hank and Charlie didn't argue, so they decided it that way. In the morning they would all mosey into or past the bank at different times, to see what guards they had. Then they'd compare notes later in one of the saloons.

As they returned to the boardinghouse, they looked for and found the office of the local law, a deputy sheriff. The office was on a sidestreet some distance from the bank. The deputy's name was Garber, according to the small sign on the door. Miz Lott told them he was the only lawman in town. "He's a nice young man," she said. "Very polite . . ."

"Does he have a deputy?"

"No. There was some talk about askin' the sheriff for another man, but I dunno what happened to that."

Breakfast cost them fifteen cents each, then they went into town in the middle of the morning, in time to see the bank open for business. Dutch joined a number of businessmen and entered the bank to look around. There were four teller's windows in a row, a low railing with a gate that fenced off several men at desks, and a row of small offices at the back, all the doors partway open.

He could see no guard.

He went down the street to the first saloon, got a stein of beer and a deck of cards, and laid out a solitaire game on a back table. Hank Betts joined him after half an hour. He hadn't seen a guard, either.

Both Charlie and Will reported the same. Charlie said, "Folks is pouring money into that goddam bank. They must got a hell of a big safe to hold it."

Hank rubbed his hands together. "When d'we take it, Dutch?"

"Let's do it tomorrow morning."

Late that afternoon they bought food and supplies and left the sacks in the stable. In the morning they rolled their blankets, paid Mrs. Lott, telling her they were heading east, and rode into town.

From a block away they watched the bank open and the first press of businessmen go in and come out. Dutch said, "Now it's our turn."

They walked the horses to the door, got down and

flipped reins over the hitchrack, and strolled inside. Dutch was in the lead. A man in a store suit was saying good-bye to a teller. He turned, nearly bumped into Dutch, said, "Beg your pardon, sir," circled Dutch, and went out.

Hank and Will walked to the other teller's cages; Charlie stood by the door. Dutch pulled his pistol and thumped the butt on the teller's ledge. "This is a holdup!"

The man squeaked, "What!"

Charlie closed the door of the bank, shooting the bolt. He went through the little gate as the men at the desks rose in surprise. One said, "What's going on?"

Charlie showed them his pistol. "This is a holdup. You-all get into that office." He pointed with the gun.

Hank herded the tellers into another of the offices. Will was filling sacks with money at the open safe. When he closed the door, Charlie ran to help Will.

Dutch stood by the little gate. "Hurry up—hurry up—"

Hank turned from the door after shoving the tellers inside, in time to see the man come from the end office. He was a portly man in a gray suit and he had a .45 Colt in his hand. Hank yelled.

The man's shot hit Dutch just above the ear, snapping his head around and taking off a large chunk of skull. Blood and tissue spattered as Hank fired three times, slamming the man against the wall. The Colt went flying, and the man crumpled, arms slack.

"What the hell!" Charlie yelled.

Dutch was dead. Hank knew it at a glance. "Get out—get out! Grab what you got and let's get out!"

They spilled from the bank and climbed on the horses. People were halting in the street—probably they had heard the shots—staring as they galloped toward the bridge. Someone fired at them, and Hank emptied the pistol over his shoulder.

Then they were on the bridge, clattering across. Jesus! Dutch was dead!

On the first rise, several miles from the town, they halted and looked back. Everything was peaceful: there was no pursuit.

"Hell, we took 'em by surprise," Charlie said. "How did Dutch get dead?"

Hank told them. "One of them bank fellers started yelling and shooting. Dutch looked around and the goddam bullet went right through 'is ear."

"It musta been the bank owner," Will said.

The money was in gray canvas sacks with leather thongs around the tops. Hank said, "C'mon. Let's git where we can count it."

They rode to the badlands and found a convenient niche to hole up in. That evening before dark, they counted the money carefully. Nine thousand dollars.

Will said, "We left three times that much. . . ."

"And Dutch," Charlie offered.

"Yeh, and Dutch." Hank scratched his jaw. "Dutch's body bound to lead the law back to Aaron. Hell, ever'body knew Dutch worked for him."

Charlie asked, "How much Aaron going to pay us?"

Hank Betts fingered the greenbacks as he stuffed them into the sacks. He glanced around at them. "Not as much as we got right here."

"They's three thousand apiece here," Will remarked. "How long since any o'you had three thousand dollars in cash?"

"Jesus—you know what you're sayin'?" Hank moved uneasily.

"'Course I know."

Charlie said, "I never had that much. I never even had a

goddamn thousand dollars all in one handful. Not in my whole life!"

Will smoothed a money sack lovingly. "I ain't got a thing back there at Madison—well, maybe a pair of pants. But this here kale will buy a lot of pants."

Charlie said, "You talking divvy up?"

"Divvy up and scatter." Will nodded.

"I dunno," Hank said. "If Aaron finds out—hell, he'll know what we done soon's we don't show up."

"What's he gonna do? Stamp around and yell," Will said. "You figger he gonna send somebody after us? Who he gonna send?"

"Howie."

Will made a rude noise. "Which one he gonna chase? We scatter and he'll give it up. We change our names, and he'll never find us."

"All right," Hank said. "We all for it?" He looked at them and they nodded.

"Let's divvy it up," Charlie said, grinning.


The government contract investigators at the end of the spur track were diligent and hard-working. They forgot about Sundays and worked from sunup to sundown. And found nothing of value.

They explored every mine hole in the area. After three weeks' work they had to admit their theory was wrong.

Reluctantly they fired the men and returned crestfallen to Fort Gillespie to report to Colonel Harrison. But Harrison was disgusted with the two and had his adjutant interview them. Major Jennings took their report without comment and sent them away.

Harrison wrote to Washington that the two were obviously inept and probably stupid.

124

★

# Chapter 19

Paul Nicholson showed the item in the *Democrat,* the local newspaper, to Jessica. Four men had held up a bank in a small town, Corona, and one of the robbers had been killed. His name was Harold 'Dutch' Bradshaw. According to the item, Bradshaw had been wearing a concho belt.

Paul said, "You and Ki had a concho that came off a belt, didn't you?"

"We still have it." She read the newspaper story. Could there be two men named Dutch Bradshaw? Not likely. Ki thought the same when she met him.

"Aaron Madison sent them to rob the bank," Ki said. He studied the item. "They didn't get much, only nine thousand. But they killed the bank president. And a posse lost them in some badlands."

Colonel Harrison suggested they go to Corona and make sure their concho matched the belt. "It'll be one more nail

125

in Madison's coffin. I think you're right that Bradshaw was one of Madison's killers."

The colonel would send cavalry immediately to keep order in Coopersville, as a stopgap. The troop now at the Northstar Mine could probably be pulled out and sent to the troubled area. Presence of the soldiers, Harrison said, would stop any sort of depredations by Madison.

A stageline took Jessica and Ki to Corona, a river town. It was a long, roundabout route that took three dusty days over terrible roads, and they both wished a hundred times they had gone across country on horseback. They arrived in Corona well after dark. The stage company put them up in its cubicle rooms, and they slept till long past sunup the next morning.

After breakfast they went to the Parker Trust Bank; it had just reopened after the robbery and murder of its president and founder, George Titus.

The founder's son, Edgar Titus, met them; he was now acting president, he told them, until the board met again.

"How can I help you?"

Ki asked, "Did any of the bank employees recognize any of the four robbers?"

"No," Titus said. "And they were all asked that question, specifically. The men were strangers to us."

"We are told the dead robber was wearing a concho belt. Where is that belt now?"

"As far as I know, Deputy Ingram has it—and the other effects of the dead man. Unless they've been claimed."

They went to see the deputy, a tall, well set-up young man with a black mustache and piercing dark eyes. No, the effects had not been claimed by anyone. He examined their credentials and brought out a box containing Bradshaw's clothes, pistol, and pocket articles.

"Bradshaw's horse was still at the hitchrack in front of

the bank when I got there," he said. "Them others didn't try t'take it with them. They was in a powerful hurry."

"He had a rifle?" Jessie asked.

"Yes." The deputy lifted it down from a shelf, an ordinary .44 Winchester.

"Will you fire that rifle please, and give us the brass?" She explained why they wanted it.

Ingram nodded, took the rifle into the street, and fired into the sky three times. He picked up the brass and handed it to her.

When the silver concho belt was laid out on a table, Ki took out the concho he had found at the Northstar massacre site and laid it by the belt. It matched exactly. There was a space on the leather belt where a concho was missing.

They explained to Ingram how they had come by the concho and what they suspected.

"We'll make a report to Colonel Harrison. He will probably write to your sheriff requesting Bradshaw's possessions. They may be needed later at a trial."

Ingram promised to keep them safe.

The three bank robbers had led the deputy and his posse on a long chase, he said. The three had run into the nearby badlands, and the tracks showed they had separated, an old Indian trick. Ingram had kept after them for four days, until their water began to give out. Then the posse had gone home.

There was nothing to do but return to Fort Gillespie. Colonel Harrison had Major Jennings send off a letter to the sheriff asking him to forward Bradshaw's things. The sheriff could keep the horse.

Then Harrison sent them back to Coopersville.

Libby Fillmore came to Madison on the noon stage. She was unimpressed with the little burg as she stepped down

127

with a hatbox in her hand. She had been told that Madison was the largest town in the territory. But as she gazed along the main street, the picture in her mind faded quickly, replaced by stern reality. This was a one-horse town.

The driver tossed down her small trunk, and she hired a boy to carry it to the Bandbox Theatre, not far down the street. The theater was next door to the Cartwheel Saloon and dancehall. Libby Fillmore was a dancer.

She was an exceedingly comely young woman, dark, with large expressive eyes and a pouting mouth. She was very well put together, as one Eastern rag had noticed. She danced in tights, which made that fact obvious.

The saloon and dancehall was owned by Aaron Madison and managed by Nate Hoyt. The theater was owned and run by Byron Houdek. Libby had been seduced into coming to Madison by Houdek's letters, offering her star roles in his productions. As she stood in front of the theater and looked at the posters, she realized she had not inquired deeply enough into what kind of productions he had talked about.

The current play offered to the public was called, *A Maiden's Lament*, and featured a scantily clad young lady who seemed to enjoy her work.

When she went inside, carpenters and other workmen were building a set on stage. A young man pointed out Byron Houdek, who came to greet her, arms outstretched. "My dear, I am overjoyed to see you! How beautiful you are! Your photographs do not do you justice."

"Thank you, Mr. Houdek."

"Byron, my love. Call me Byron, please." He took her into his office and closed the door. "We will put you up at Mrs. Louden's Boardinghouse. I will see you get the best room in her establishment. As you saw, we are readying a new play in which you will star! Rehearsals start in about three days. . . . I will have the sides in your hands by this evening."

And he did. He sent her to the boardinghouse escorted by his assistant, Jerome, and the next day she met the other cast members; the new play was called *Betrayed!* Libby would play the "other" woman.

Publicity went out from Houdek's office, extolling the virtues and beauty of his new star, and this material came to Aaron Madison's attention at once.

He came to view a rehearsal and meet Libby and was entranced by her. She quickly learned he was the most important man she was ever likely to meet, and allowed him to carry her off to his hilltop fort where he wined and dined her—and did his best to get her into his bed.

She fought him off.

Perhaps it would have been better had she not. It only whetted his appetite. He had to have her! He offered twice her salary to come and work for him in the Cartwheel dancehall as a singer. She refused and he doubled the offer.

When he doubled it again, she relented. When Houdek was able to replace her in the play, she moved her charms next door. Libby was a dancer; her singing was borderline at best, but she wore her tights and no one complained. Least of all Aaron. He stood in the wings every night to watch and had champagne shipped from the East for their little suppers in a private room upstairs.

She held out valiantly, but was overpowered. Aaron got her into bed quickly, when he set his mind to it. She was now his, one of his possessions. He let everyone know it, by words and actions.

Libby was appalled by what she had allowed to happen, and could not change. Aaron was not her idea of a leading man. She wanted out.

But she soon learned that Aaron did not give up his

possessions easily—if at all. She was his, like it or not. So was the town, and so was the territory. What was that song . . . ? She was a bird in a gilded cage.

Each night she cried bitter tears into her pillow. Could she escape?

The land about Coopersville was range country. In the eyes of Aaron Madison, the town was a running sore. It served him no purpose, brought strangers across the range, and would be better off gone.

His plans were to eliminate it entirely. After the people were removed, he would have crews tear the buildings down and salvage what lumber they could. The rest would be burned, as it had been at Markey. In a few years no one would know a town had stood there.

Except that some people called it home. They did not want to move away. They had bought the land their homes stood on and it belonged to them—not Aaron Madison.

They were the stubborn ones.

One of them was Ira Foster. He was in his fifties, a grizzled and untidy man who eked out a living chopping wood, hauling goods, and doing odd jobs. His wife had long since gone to her reward, and his children had grown and moved out.

Ira was one of those Jessica and Ki talked to when they investigated Coopersville. Ira swore that Madison's men had told him they were going to destroy the town. "They got orders to burn 'er down."

"Orders from whom?"

"From Aaron Madison. He the one pays their wages."

They also talked to others, but of all the people who swore Madison was behind the plans to destroy the town, only one, Ira Foster, was willing to put down in writing what he had seen, heard, and knew, with names, places, and dates.

"I got no one t'worry about me," he said. "Them others has got wives an' families."

The troop of cavalry was busy patrolling the area, showing themselves, and while they were very evident, there was no trouble. No gangs of armed men rode into the town; no threats were made.

The troop commander made his daily reports to Colonel Harrison, who in turn reported to Washington.

Washington decided that since the area was quiet, the troop could be withdrawn—over the protests of Colonel Harrison, who stated that the lawlessness would continue the moment the cavalry departed.

The Secretary of War replied that the army was not a police force, and that since the late war the army had been drastically reduced in size. There were not enough troops to spare for every minor or local insurrection. The U.S. Marshals, county sheriffs, and other police would have to control the situations with the help of the courts.

The cavalry was ordered back to Fort Gillespie.

Three days later Ira Foster was shot and killed in a corral outside of Coopersville . . . by persons unknown.

# Chapter 20

Jessica and Ki were south of the town and learned of the shooting late in the afternoon. A half dozen men were standing around the body of the old man, waiting for a wagon.

No one had seen the shooting, but most had heard the shots. Everyone agreed there had been three shots fired. Ira had not been armed.

"Which way did the killer go?" Ki asked.

No one knew. A man said, "He didn't go into town. I was comin' from the store. I woulda seen him."

Another said, "He didn't go east, neither. I woulda seen 'im."

"Then he went west or north?"

"Must have . . ."

They rode west, looking for tracks on the prairie sod. Jessie thought the killer would probably circle south and go back to Madison. Could the man be other than one of Madison's killers?

Jessica was grim-lipped. "He was a harmless old man, going about his daily chores. And somebody shot him down in cold blood. . . . "

"Madison plays for keeps."

"He murders for keeps, you mean."

"Yes . . ."

When night fell they continued west for several hours and halted on a rise of 'ground. There was always the chance that someone would get careless with a fire. . . . But they saw nothing.

In the morning they turned south and halted on high ground to survey the land with binoculars. "A rider!" Ki exclaimed in surprise. He pointed and Jessie focused the glasses.

"He doesn't see us. I see only one rider. . . . "

"Yes, he's alone. Let's try to close."

But in an hour they had come no closer to the man, and they suspected he had detected them. They moved wide apart and continued the chase. About midday the man was bending eastward, and in the middle of the afternoon they came on a range of low hills and jumbled earth, and had to move more slowly for fear of ambush.

The other's tracks were easy to follow however; the earth was softer. Ki took a rifle and went ahead on foot, taking advantage of every bit of cover. In a deep ravine he drew fire and dropped full length on the sand. The shot had come from the lip of the ravine, perhaps fifty yards farther on. Cradling the Winchester, he drew a bead on a clump of brush near where he'd seen smoke, and waited. When the brush moved slightly, Ki fired into the middle of it. The brush moved violently for a few seconds, then was still.

Had he hit the other?

He waited a few minutes, then moved forward and climbed out of the draw to lay flat, searching the land with his eyes. Crawling to the bit of brush, he found nothing. He swore under his breath.

He located the tracks again and followed them cautiously and did not draw fire again for almost an hour. Then a shot ricocheted off a rock just above his head. The lead screamed into space as Ki ducked low. He spotted the smoke in a cleft of rocks ahead but could see no movement.

By the time he reached the rocks, he could see the open prairie again. The rider was loping his horse half a mile distant, moving southeast.

Ki whistled—the whistle that meant "danger past"— and in a short while Jessie showed up with the horses.

They followed the rider until dusk. Jessie was positive the man was pointing for Madison. Ki agreed, but was also sure the man would change direction after dark.

Jessie said, "Why don't we go on till we're close to the town and wait for him?"

Ki made a face. "As good as any. . . ."

They walked the horses in near darkness for hours, halting when they saw the lights of the little town glimmering ahead, probably half a dozen miles away. They could not be sure the man they pursued had not already gone into the town, but if he had changed direction at dusk, to confuse them, then they were possibly between him and the town.

"He'll start shooting at sight of us," Ki said. "Keep a sharp lookout."

The remainder of the night passed slowly, and with the gray dawn the rider appeared, off to their left. Ki saw him first and fired three quick shots. But the man had seen him and anticipated the shots, turning away like the wind, sending a shot back as he fled.

Jessica spurred to keep between him and the town; Ki followed directly. The light was tricky, still gray and uncertain, and the man disappeared.

Ki galloped the horse to the spot he'd last seen the fugitive and found nothing. He could see Jessie off to his right; the man had not gone that way.

Then he stumbled onto the arroyo. Obviously the man had known about it. It was a deep ravine, rather narrow, and lined with thick brush. The man had gone down into it and backtracked. Ki swore as he found the spot where the horse had slid down to the sandy bottom.

He whistled to Jessie. Their quarry had gotten away.

Aaron Madison read about the Corona robbery and murder in the newspaper, and swore at Dutch's death. He had lost a good man.

But where were the other three? They should have returned long since . . . with the money. The paper said nine thousand. When a week passed he knew they had gone off with it. Without Dutch to hold them together they had reverted to type. Aaron raged: they had robbed him!

They had robbed him at exactly the wrong time. He needed cash desperately. Every penny that came in went out immediately.

Ambrose Coyle was enlisting men, and they had to be paid in cash. If not they would desert.

And he had five wagons full of gold ore, sitting. Sitting! And he had to pay men to guard them! He paced the office and swore, chewing on a cigar.

There had to be men who would buy the ore as it was— if he could find them. And the only way was to ask. He halted and stood at the window, seeing nothing of the out-

135

side. Who could he send? What about Walter Simon, who ran the saddle shop with his son? Walter had been a prospector and knew something about ore—probably more than anyone else in town.

Snapping his fingers, he went outside and sent a boy for Walter.

Howie returned from Coopersville that day and came to report. He had looked over the situation at Coopersville and seen the cavalry depart.

"They jest up and packed the tents one day and skedaddled."

"That's fine . . ."Aaron rubbed his hands together. "You came back sooner than I expected. Did you have trouble with the army?"

"No—had to get out, though," Howie explained. "Old Ira Foster, he was gettin' mouthy—"

"You shot him?"

Howie shrugged. "They wan't anything I could do else. But the sodjers was three days gone. Nobody seen it. What the hell."

Aaron sat down behind the desk and eyed the lean man. "Three days?"

"I hung around because the blond woman and the Chinaman was there, hopin' I could get a shot at one of 'em."

"And did you?"

Howie sighed and shook his head. "Them two is like shadows. Quick as cats. And one of 'em is allus guardin' the other's back."

"Go on . . ."

"Well, like I said, Ira been talkin' against us, so I follered him to an old corral north of town and fixed 'is wagon . . . and damn if that Chinaman and the blond woman didn't show up. I was alone and they didn't see

136

me, so I lit out west. They musta follered my tracks—"

"You didn't lead them here, did you!?" Aaron frowned.

"No, hell no. I lost 'em out on the flats. They got no idee where I went."

"How can you be sure?"

"I watched for 'em."

"All right. Get some men together and go back to Coopersville. You know what to do."

Howie nodded.

Jessica and Ki made camp several miles from town, where they could see the pale glimmer of lantern light. They waited till full dark, listening to the owls hunting. It was foolish not to make another search for the rolled-up pages from Aaron's ledger now that they were so close.

The sliver of moon had gone when they rode close to the hill fort; they left the horses in a draw and walked carefully through sooty shadows to the grassy area under the dark log walls.

This time they moved farther around the hill, though Ki believed it was too far. . . . They spent more than an hour on hands and knees, listening to the mutter of voices on the wall so close by.

And then Jessica found the tightly rolled papers!

She gave a squealing little cry, quickly muffled, but one of the sentries called to another, and they heard louder conversation as they hurried away, but no shots were fired.

They decided to take the papers to Colonel Harrison at once.

★

# Chapter 21

Libby Fillmore had only one weapon in her arsenal to use against Aaron Madison. Her wiles.

She used them first on Wilbur Dunning. Slinky arms about his thin neck, pressing her warm body against him, lips at his ear, "Will you help me, Willy?"

"H-help you do what?"

She took a long breath, undulating against him. "To get away from Aaron."

He grabbed her and pushed her away. "Are you trying to get me killed!?" He ran out of the room and slammed the door.

Disgusted, Libby threw herself on the bed. He was a little rabbit, afraid of his shadow. Were all Aaron's people deathly afraid of him? Well, not all. She had seen Howie and some of the others like him, but *she* was afraid of them. One of them might ride off with her, but what would he do when they were alone? She shuddered. She did not want the fire immediately after the frying pan.

But there were people who did not work for Aaron. Next door, in fact, there were several actors who might be receptive. . . . What about young Logan Ellis? He had seemed very interested in her—she had felt his eyes on her. He had a daredevil glint in his eyes, and he was no weakling.

How could she meet him to talk about it?

She was singing at the Cartwheel, but not every moment. The saloon had a greenroom of sorts at the rear of the building, with a rear door. She might easily slip next door to the theater for a few moments now and then, on some pretext—watching a rehearsal, perhaps. Byron Houdek wouldn't mind, she was certain. She might then catch Logan's eye. . . .

Aaron took her to the dancehall about dusk each day. She then put on her costume while he worked in the office upstairs. She had perhaps fifteen minutes to herself—not a very long period. The first time she slipped next door, she had barely time for a few words with Byron and hardly time to flutter her lashes at Logan.

She was surprised then, an hour later, to see him standing in the wings as she sang several songs.

He was gone when she came offstage; he must have come in during the play's intermission. It made her smile. It was a first step.

The second step occurred the next evening when, as she opened the rear door of the greenroom, he was standing only a few feet away, seemingly deep in thought.

"Oh—Logan—" she said, a hand to her throat.

He smiled. "I was wondering if you were on yet."

"I go on in about ten minutes."

He came close and took her hand. "You don't belong in a dancehall, you know."

139

"It's kind of you to say it."

He squeezed her hand. "Byron has hinted that you were lured away by enormous wages."

"Yes . . . I suppose that's true."

He took a breath. "Are you—I mean—" He cleared his throat. "Are you that man's mistress?"

She stiffened. "I am a prisoner."

He was astonished. "A prisoner!?"

"Yes. I am watched and never allowed outside—this moment is stolen, in fact."

"How can that be?"

"It is a fact! And I wish very much to go away from here!" She looked toward the door. "I must go inside. They must not find me here."

His face showed his astonishment. He opened the door for her, and she glided inside and closed it, heart thumping. Had she overdone it?

No—she *was* a prisoner! It was the truth. But would he believe her? More to the point, would he help her? Should she have been more direct . . . promised something . . . ?

Well, she would find out soon.

He slipped into the dancehall again, during the play's intermission. She saw him in the wings for several moments as she sang. What was he thinking?

The next evening she talked to him for a few minutes outside the greenroom door. He said, "I'm leaving in a few days—the play will finish its run in two days. Why don't you come with me to the railroad? I'll get a buggy—"

"It's dangerous!"

He made a face. "He can't keep you here against your will!"

"But he has been! You don't know him!"

He looked at her curiously. "I'm offering you a chance to go East. Have you any money?"

"Yes, yes . . . but I'm afraid."

"Bosh. Come with me. You'll be safe enough."

His words ran through her mind over and over that night. Was Aaron all bluff? Logan seemed to think so. How could he hold her prisoner!

What would she take with her? A small valise should do it. She packed it and put it aside where he would not notice it, and she talked with Logan again. He was very sure of himself, and his confidence extended to her. They would go north to the railroad and take the train east. It was that simple. Let Aaron Madison shout. What could he do?

There was the problem of *when* to go. She was whirled away to the hill fort each night after the show.

He said, "Then we'll go during the show. You will simply disappear. No one will know where you've gone. You haven't told anyone about our plans, have you?"

"Certainly not! No one."

"Good. I'll wait in the buggy in the alley behind the dancehall. When you come out, we'll go, and they'll never find us."

Her heart was thumping. When she saw Aaron he seemed to look through her, but she knew it was her own fear, and she forced the feelings down. She watched him go upstairs and began to feel better. Logan was right; they wouldn't know where to look for her.

In the middle of the evening she came offstage as a bevy of dancers ran out to the shouts of the crowd. Quickly she grabbed a cape and her valise and slipped out to the alley. Logan was there, as he'd promised, grinning at her. She climbed into the light buggy and they were off.

He was right. It was easy!

They traveled all that night, following a ghost of a road. It was cold and she huddled in her cape, staring at the misty hills, unable to sleep because of the constant jolting.

Logan told her he was going to Philadelphia, where he'd been offered a job with a traveling company. He suggested she come along, too. "They're sure to hire a beautiful girl like you."

She would think about it. She had about a hundred dollars saved. Madison owed her more, but she would never collect it now.

It was about an hour after sunup when Logan, glancing back, saw the dust. Riders were coming after them.

When he mentioned it to Libby, she became very agitated. "Go faster! Can't you go faster!?"

He tried, but the horse and buggy could not outrun horsemen. They caught up within the hour, two men she had seen in the saloon. One grabbed the reins and pulled the buggy to a halt.

Logan stood up, a small pistol in his hand. "You have no right to stop us!"

Libby screamed as the second man shot him. The pistol barked twice, and Logan fell to his knees and tumbled to the ground. She saw the splash of blood on his white shirt ... the world began to waver and grow hazy and she slumped on the seat.

The killer said, "She done fainted, for crissakes."


The cut-out pages were in good condition after having lain out in the weeds for weeks. Ki had rolled them tightly, and the dew had not affected them. They spread them out under sheets of glass and studied them.

The book they came from had obviously been Aaron Madison's private journal ... not intended for other eyes. The dates and amounts of money jibed with the robberies.

"It's good," Colonel Harrison said. "But it isn't proof that Madison did the robberies. But taken with everything

142

else I believe a jury would convict him. *If* we could get him into a court."

"An honest court," Jessie said.

"I believe we can prove that the man, Dutch Bradshaw, worked for Madison. That's another nail."

Ki asked, "What about the brass from Bradshaw's rifle?"

The colonel shrugged. "They didn't match. It wasn't his rifle, unfortunately. The sheriff agreed to turn over Bradshaw's effects, and they're on the way here."

The Coopersville situation was under control, Harrison told them. He had sent an officer and several men to organize the remaining residents into a defensive force and there had been no other murders.

Madison, the Colonel thought, was being contained.

Jessica and Ki returned to Hanover, not at all sure that he was right. They were no closer to getting the man into a federal court to answer for his crimes.


The two, Hank Betts and Slim Reher, turned the buggy around and headed back to Madison, leaving the body of Logan in the road.

Libby came around soon after and sat mute on the seat in a state of shock. Logan had been murdered before her eyes. She saw the bullets slam into him and saw him fall a hundred times on the return journey. Logan had been terribly wrong about Aaron.

And they had callously left his body in the road.

It was a different world than she'd been used to, a world where life was cheap—and they were taking her back to it. She had never felt so utterly hopeless.

When she saw Aaron, he only stared at her and turned away. But that night he pushed his way into her bed. Her tears did not stop him; he paid no attention to them.

143

After he had gone she lay awake staring into the gloom. She had to get away from this place . . . but how? She had done no real planning with Logan; he had been so sure of himself.

The next time she must plan carefully. It had to be possible. It *had* to be.


Aaron had sent a boy for Walter Simon, who had prospecting experience and knew about gold ore.

The boy returned to say that Walter had died several months ago.

Aaron swore.

★

# Chapter 22

While they had been at Coopersville, Colonel Harrison had been busy. Without consulting anyone—for fear of a leak at the fort—he had met with several men and picked one for a dangerous mission. None of the men knew the mission when they met in secret.

The man the colonel selected, Roy Stevens, a corporal of engineers, was highly intelligent, youthful in appearance, and not easily shaken up, as his record confirmed.

He volunteered for the mission when it was revealed to him, and set out immediately, dressed as a cowhand looking for work, down on his luck. He went to Madison and hung out in saloons, listening, remembering. . . .

He would have to ride to Norris to send a wire in an emergency. Otherwise he would meet another man who would come from the fort and meet Stevens outside the town for Stevens's report each week. Stevens was a spy.

Jessica and Ki were surprised when Colonel Harrison

appeared in Hanover and came to Jessica's room late at night, asking her to rap on Ki's door.

When he dressed and came in, the colonel locked the door and told them about Stevens, without mentioning his name.

"He has been in Madison a week, and his first report is very interesting. Aaron Madison is leaving—or perhaps has already left—for Fargo. It's a town on the Kansas and Fort Stanton Railroad."

"That's nearly two hundred miles from here!" Jessie said. "Does your man know why he's going?"

"No. I'm going to wire the U.S. Marshal to apprehend him. And I want you to go there also. This is a chance to corral him and bring him to justice."

Jessie looked at Ki. She said, "We'll leave at once."

"Good." Harrison clenched his fists. "Maybe we'll get him this time!"


Aaron Madison was annoyed. The four senators he had written to had obviously gotten together and refused as a group to come to Madison. It was too far, they said. And two were up for re-election and had to be in their home states to campaign. They could not be gone that long, or chance losing to a challenger.

They suggested meeting at Fargo. It was on the railroad, and they could travel there with speed and in comfort.

Madison had to agree. It was a long, tedious journey for him, but of course the senators were not interested in *his* comfort.

He made his preparations; he would travel in his own coach and take along Wilbur Dunning to make his life easier with household chores.

And to make sure Libby Fillmore did not try to run off again, he left Troy Garnitz in charge of her. Troy could be trusted to watch her every move and yet not be officious. He was a softspoken man, hard as nails, a former saloon bouncer. She would not outguess him.

Aaron had plans for Troy; he could move easily into the job once filled by Dutch Bradshaw. Dutch's passing had left a gap.

For her part, Libby was disconsolate when she realized Aaron was leaving and Troy was her bodyguard . . . and keeper. He watched her when she sang on stage, and he was outside the greenroom door when she opened it . . . and closed it again. The next time she tried to open it, it had been locked from the outside.

Now she was really a prisoner.


Jessica and Ki traveled to Fargo at once. They took the stage to Westbrook, a hundred-mile journey, then boarded the train which took them to Fargo two days later. They arrived in the morning to find Fargo a bustling town.

They put up at one of the four hotels and looked up the U.S. Marshal at once. His name, according to the gold leaf on the office door, was Cyril Holmes. Inside, a clerk informed them that Marshal Holmes was away, that they could see Deputy John Regan.

Regan was a tall young man with quick eyes and an easy manner. He seated them in his tiny office, saying a letter had been received from Colonel Harrison, mentioning them.

"I am sorry Marshal Holmes is not here. I'm afraid you'll have to put up with me."

"I'm sure you'll do very well," Jessie said, measuring him. Regan wore a vest that strained itself across a broad chest. He looked competent to handle a great many jobs. . . .

They discussed Aaron Madison. Regan said, "Colonel

Harrison believes we have enough evidence to convict Madison in federal court. Have you seen this evidence?"

"We know about it," Jessie said, nodding. "The payroll robberies and killings, the Northstar massacre, and the affair at Corona, for instance."

"Yes. The colonel says these were all masterminded by Madison."

"Undoubtedly. And others, too."

Regan asked, "Why is he coming here?"

"We don't know. Can you find out which hotel he will stay in?"

Regan nodded. "Easily. And you want me to take him into custody?"

"Yes—but not at once. Let's find out, if we can, why he's here."

"Yes. Good idea. We've got some people who are good at that. I'll put them on it."


As Aaron had surmised, it was impossible to keep the news from the press that four United States senators were in town. Reporters wanted to know why. And they were given a well-concocted story about committees and land development and farm problems. . . . The senators' aides made the handouts as dull as possible, hoping the news factor would be diminished . . . and it appeared to be.

None of the senators gave interviews and all four stayed in their suites in the Alexander Hotel, never appearing in public.

Aaron Madison also stayed at the Alexander and made himself as inconspicuous as possible.

But Deputy Regan's people easily discovered that Madison and the senators were having constant meetings, some into the small hours of the morning.

They could not learn why.

After three days the meetings apparently stopped.

The next day Deputy Regan and four men went to Aaron Madison's suite and rapped on the door. No one answered.

The suite was empty.

Their business concluded for the moment, and agreements arrived at, Aaron left the hotel at three in the morning. He rolled out of town in his coach, taking the road east. If anyone were watching, this was the most unlikely road. According to the map, he could turn south, then west, and hopefully throw off any pursuit.

His supposition was correct.

Regan's men dashed pell-mell along the road west, thinking to overtake Madison in hours. After a day's ride they were still looking at an empty road and a vacant horizon. If Aaron Madison had come this way, he was flying low and they would never catch him.

They straggled back to town to report. Aaron had stolen a march on them.

"It's embarrassing," Ki said. "He's outguessed us again."

# Chapter 23

Byron Houdek received a play from the east, in a bundle of mail, and put it aside for several weeks. It was a play he was not particularly familiar with, *A Maiden's Fortunes,* though he had seen it performed in Baltimore during a visit there.

When he read it again, he was struck how admirably Libby Fillmore might play the heroine, Elisa. She was perfect for the role. It was also the kind of play he was certain his rough, untutored audiences would love. It might run for months and net him a nice bundle of cash.

He went at once to see Aaron Madison.

He had to wait for a week till Madison returned—they did not tell him from where—but then Madison received him in the upstairs office. "What is it, Houdek?"

Byron explained about the play and how perfect Libby would be as the star.

Aaron stared at him during the recital. "How well do you know Libby?"

Byron was surprised at the question. "Not well at all. She came to the theater asking for a job, and I gave her one, and then you hired her away." He shrugged. "I would like to cast her in this role because she fits it physically, that's all."

"You know of course that she tried to run off with one of your actors. . . . "

"I had nothing to do with it. As you know, actors are a curious lot. Most of them have the morals of a tomcat. I refuse to be held accountable for any of them."

Aaron sniffed. "How can I be sure it won't happen again?"

"Station a man backstage."

"Have you talked to Libby about this?"

"No. I came to you first."

Aaron rubbed his jaw. The idea of seeing Libby, the woman he was bedding, in a role on a stage was appealing to him. He could easily put a man to make sure she did not run off again. He said, "Very well, I will talk to her."

He discussed the idea with her that night, and she was delighted. She was disgusted with the saloon and its customers who occasionally shot off six-guns in the middle of her act; she would never get used to that. When she complained to Nate Hoyt, the saloon manager, he told her it was simple exuberance. She had never heard shooting in the theater next door. It would be a welcome change.

Libby read the script and showed up on the appointed day, accompanied by Hank Betts, who was to keep an eye on her. She detested him and protested to Aaron, but he only smiled. "If you want to perform in the play, you will abide by my rules."

Betts did not intrude upon her, and after several days she forgot he was there.

The cast comprised four others, another and older woman, and three men. One of the men was Jodie Wiggins, a rather handsome leading man whose eyes seemed constantly to be on her.

Byron Houdek blocked the play, and the rehearsals went on daily. When they were given rest periods. Jodie attempted to talk to her, but Hank Betts was always close by, listening. It discouraged conversation.

Roy Stevens, with orders to report all happenings in Madison, duly noted the new play and Libby Fillmore's role in it, mentioning that Libby was Aaron Madison's mistress.

This was news to Jessica, Ki, and Colonel Harrison. How could they use this knowledge to their advantage? Ki suggested at once that they kidnap Libby and perhaps get Aaron to leave his stronghold.

"Won't he send a gang of men to get her back?" Jessie asked.

"Probably. But will he lead them himself?"

Colonel Harrison thought not.

He also instructed Roy Stevens, by way of the intermediary, to get in touch with Libby Fillmore if that were at all possible.

Stevens was a slim, smooth-faced young man who made himself look hangdog. He enjoyed his role as spy and entered into it as enthusiastically as a stage actor in a big city production. Upon receiving the colonel's suggestion, he went to the Bandbox Theatre, asking to do odd jobs and was given a broom.

He swept out the theater, the backstage areas, found that many of the theater seats needed repairing, and brought this to Houdek's attention, so was able to stay on. In this manner he met the cast and was tolerated by the members. He did them favors and quickly saw that Libby had a bodyguard-keeper who seldom let her out of his sight. Roy Stevens became such a familiar figure backstage that no one, not even Hank Betts, gave him second glances.

But he was never able to have any kind of conversation with Libby.

When rehearsals were finished, the play went on for the public, and Aaron Madison attended the opening night. It was the first time Stevens had seen him. He came into the theater with two obvious gunmen, one on each side, and sat in the fifth row center.

Immediately following opening night, the leading man, Jodie Wiggins, hosted a cast party in the hotel, and after the final curtain the cast whirled off in several buggies, leaving Hank Betts behind. He had not been told of the party and did not expect it. The cast, in fact, took great joy in evading and foiling him, hustling Libby out of the dressing room dressed as a man.

When Betts realized he had been duped and that Libby was not where she was supposed to be, he ran to inform Aaron Madison.

Aaron organized a quick search, discovered the party, and went there himself in a rage to pull Libby from its midst, and threaten Byron Houdek in front of everyone.

His action put a damper on the party, and it broke up very soon. But it informed the cast and everyone connected to the theater of the situation that Libby found herself in. She was in real fact a prisoner.

And now that her situation was common knowledge, she confessed that she would do almost anything to get away from Madison. The entire cast set about devising plans for her to do just that.

Roy Stevens reported all of this to Colonel Harrison,

saying that it was his belief that if she went, Aaron would go after her himself, in person, as he had to the hotel.

Jessica and Ki, evading Paul Nicholson, rode at once to the vicinity of Madison and met Stevens at night with the contact from the fort, a middle-aged sergeant.

It was Roy Stevens's opinion that Aaron Madison was obsessed with the girl and would do anything to keep her. "But I believe with the help of the cast people, we can get Libby away from the town."

Ki said, "You mean spirit her away in the night?"

"Yes."

Jessie shook her head. "The government is not interested in just the girl—it wants Aaron Madison. If the girl is spirited away—Madison must know about it so he can follow."

Stevens let out his breath. "That makes it twice as difficult. Madison is surrounded by killers."

"Yes," Ki said. "We would like to lead Madison into a trap, capture him, and put him into a federal court. Libby would then be one more witness against him."

"It's not going to be easy," Stevens said. "Too many things could go wrong. What kind of trap would you set?"

"Cavalry," Ki said. "Lead him into the middle of a troop."

"It's our best chance right now," Jessica said urgently. "Can you get a cast member to meet with us?"

"Yes, I think so."

"Then let's meet here tomorrow night and set a schedule."

Stevens nodded. "I'll have to tell them who I really am. . . ."

"That had to be done in any case, sooner or later."

"Yes, I know. . . ."

They sent the sergeant back to the fort to inform Colonel Harrison of their plans and to receive from him his agreement to supply the troop of cavalry where and when they wanted it.

"It all takes so much time communicating," Jessica fumed. "Two weeks will go by before we can set the plan in motion."

"There's no way to do it faster," Ki said. "I wish we had our own private telegraph wire. There will never be anything faster than that. . . ."

"But we don't." They studied a map of the terrain and decided on the spot for the cavalry. It was a rocky canyon through which the road north weaved for half a mile. A troop could easily hide itself there and surround a traveler.

They would mark the spot on the map and send it back by the sergeant on his next trip.

The next night Roy Stevens showed up with the play's leading man, Jodie Wiggins. He had been informed of the plan and was enthusiastic about it. Apparently everyone hated Aaron Madison.

But he had news that was not exactly to their liking. He had been talking privately to Libby, he told them. She did not want to try to slip away again. "She remembers the murder of Logan Ellis," Jodie said. "She still has nightmares about it. She doesn't want anyone else killed because of her."

"Is this a whim?" Jessie asked. "Or is it definite? The plan won't work without her."

"I'll have to find out," the actor said. "But she sounded very definite. Maybe I can change her mind."

"You have to change her mind!"

155

# Chapter 24

Aaron Madison sat in his office, growling to himself. He needed money. He needed cash! It was astonishing how fast ten thousand dollars disappeared into thin air. His payroll ate much of it. Ambrose Coyle was constantly warning him that he must not fall behind or he'd wind up with no armed force at all.

He had depended on the Corona enterprise seeing him through a difficult month—and it had come to nothing and Dutch gone. He needed another Corona, only successful. He needed another army payroll!

And he needed a refinery.

Fishing for a cigar, he chewed the end of it and got up to stare through the window. Why not send Howie south, a hundred miles or so, maybe in Wayne River. There were several banks in that town. Let Howie relieve the pressure with a few sacks of money.

He went downstairs to the saloon and sent one of the boys for him.

Back in his office, he lit another cigar and sat back in his chair. Robbing banks was not the best solution to his problems, but it was the only quick one. His other enterprises, such as the saloon, made money but not enough. There were always odd expenses, worn out equipment, and the like. Only yesterday, for instance, one of the hostlers had informed him that several of the wagons would have to be replaced; they had been repaired for the last time and could not be depended upon.

He sighed deeply and grunted when Howie appeared in the open doorway. "Come in and close the door."

Howie did as he was told and sat opposite the big desk.

"Do you know Wayne River?"

"I've been there," Howie said. "A while ago . . ."

Aaron outlined his plan and Howie nodded. "I'll take three men. When d'you want us to leave?"

"Right away. You ought to be back in a week. . . ."

Howie went to the door. "Right. Give or take a day." He went out.


When he met Jessica and Ki that night, Roy Stevens had more bad news. "I've just been hired by Aaron Madison."

"What!"

"One of his foremen, a man named Howie Cutler, hired me this morning."

Jessie asked, "Do you have to work for him?"

"That's the trouble! I've been hanging around town telling everyone I was down on my luck and needed a job. How's it going to look if I don't take Howie's job?"

"But you're working at the theater."

157

"Sweeping it out?" Stevens shook his head. "No, I got to take Howie's job or skedaddle."

Ki asked, "What is the job?"

"I don't know. It's somewhere out of town. We're leaving in the morning and will be gone maybe a week."

Jessie sighed.

Ki asked, "How many going out of town?"

"Only a couple, as far as I know. I'm to take a rifle and a bedroll. We'll be travelin' light."

"All right. We'll continue to meet with Jodie while you're gone. He still has to convince Libby. . . ."

When Stevens had departed, Ki looked after him. "I wonder—I wonder if they're going to rob a bank? What d'you think?"

"They could be. . . ."

"We'd better notify the colonel to warn every bank within a three-day ride from here."

Howie set a hard, steady pace that ate up the miles. They went directly south, mostly following an ancient Indian trail, then bent eastward. Just after dusk of the second day they saw the lights of a town and Howie halted, telling them to dismount.

"You-all stay here. I'll be back in an hour." He disappeared in the gloom.

Stevens asked, "Where the hell are we going anyway?"

Willie Hobart said, "We goin' to that town, Wayne River."

"Then why didn't we go in with Howie?"

Willie looked at Nate and they both chuckled. "When you work for Madison, you do like you're told, kid."

"I allus do. . . ."

"Didn't Howie tell you nothing?"

"No."

158

Nate said, "You let Howie tell 'im. It's no skin off our butt."

"Tell me what?" Stevens asked.

"Hell, he come this far," Willie said. "Howie shoulda told 'im."

"Dammit! What?"

Willie said, "We goin' to bust the bank, kid."

"Bust the bank!" Stevens stared at them. "Shit!" He felt suddenly hollow—and a little scared. He had known that Will and Nate were a couple of hard cases, but it hadn't occurred to him that they were going to rob a bank!

Nate said, "You jest do like we tell you, and it'll be finer'n snuff."

Howie was back in about an hour, and they found a place to bed down for the night. Howie said, "We'll go in just b'fore noon."

"What're we doing here?" Stevens asked.

Howie looked at him. "We're going to walk in the bank and come out with cash. You're going to stay with the horses and cover us when we come out."

Stevens stared at him. "You shoulda asked me—"

"Do like you're told, kid. Roll up and get some sleep."

There was nothing else he could do. There was no possibility of getting away in the night. He was stuck. He was going to be a bank robber! Like it or not. Jesus! Would Colonel Harrison understand he was stuck with the job?


Jodie Wiggins talked with Libby every chance he got. It was understandable that she was afraid. It must have been terrible to watch Logan Ellis shot down in cold blood . . . and his body left lying on the road.

She shuddered and turned away when Jodie mentioned getting out. "I-I don't want to talk about it."

"But you don't want to stay here, either."

"No—but—"

"You can trust these people. They're very competent."

She stared at him. "Why do you care what happens to me? Why do *they* care? I don't even know them."

He finally had to tell her it was part of a plan to get Aaron Madison out of the town so he could be taken.

"You mean you're using me for bait!"

"That's not a very pretty way to put it—"

"But it's true, isn't it? You're using me to get to Aaron." She firmed her lips. "You know he's capable of killing me if he finds out."

"He won't be able to kill you—he won't get near you. He'll be surrounded by cavalrymen. They'll take him to Fort Gillespie, and he'll stand trial for murdering and robbing, and that'll be the end of him."

She sighed deeply. "You make it sound so easy. Aaron is not stupid. He'll be very suspicious. . . ."

"That's why we're counting on you. If he thinks he's chasing you—that you've run off as you did before—"

She shuddered. "I don't want to take the chance. . . . It could happen again."

"It won't."

She almost yelled: "How can you be so sure! Can you see into the future! I don't need any more nightmares!" She ran out as he swore.

He had to report to Jessie and Ki that she was adamant. "She's afraid to do it."

"Then we've lost," Jessie said. "We need her to make it work." Her voice softened. "I can't blame her, really. . . ."

"Wait a minute," Ki said. "All is *not* lost. We can make the plan work without her."

"What? How?"

"We figure to get Aaron out of his castle to chase after Libby. He thinks he'll overtake her, and bring her back. If

160

he thinks it, then it's real for him. But it doesn't have be Libby he chases."

"Jesus!" Jodie said. "It could be me in a wig!"

"That's right. He'll be chasing Jessie. And she'll lead him right into the arms of the U.S. Cavalry."

Jessica laughed. "Marvelous!"

"We'll have to hide Libby somewhere, but that ought to be easy."

"If she agrees. . . . "

Jodie threw up his hands. "She'll have to agree!"


In the morning they walked the horses into town and had breakfast in a café across the street from one of the two banks. As they ate, Howie said to Stevens, "Stop starin' at the goddamn bank, kid. You look guilty as a horse thief."

"Well, I guess I am."

Willie laughed. "It'll be over in a minute. Don't worry about it."

When they went out to the street, Howie said, "I'll mosey into the bank and out. Willie, you go over to the other one. We want to know about guards." He pointed. "Nate, you and the kid sit in them chairs. We be back in a jiffy."

Stevens sat as he was told, and watched Howie enter the bank, strolling casually. Howie was calm as an iceberg. Stevens could feel his heart pounding. . . .

He said to Nate, "He wants me to stay with the horses. What d'I do?"

Nate made a face. "Nothin'll happen till we come out'n the bank. Nobody goin' to know we in there . . . less'n there's shootin'. If people out here on the street hear shootin' from the bank, then you might have a passel of trouble."

"You mean they'll rush the bank?"

"They prob'ly wait till we come out. It could get down-right onery. I jest hope they don't shoot the horses."

Stevens pondered that. If he were caught as part of a gang, would it mean Leavenworth Prison for him? He bit his lips. Would Nate shoot him if he tried to get away now?

He was about ready to try it when Howie came out of the bank.

Howie crossed the street and strolled toward them as if he belonged. He sat down by Nate. "No guard at all. But it's a small bank. Three people inside, far's I could see." He pulled out a sack of Durham. "Le's see what Willie got."

Will came back in about ten minutes. He stood in front of Howie, thumbs in his belt. "Two shotgun guards lookin' ever'body over good. Be a lot of shooting, we go in there."

Howie nodded. "We'll take the other one then. Roy stays outside. If there's shootin', look out for folks with rifles, but we'll come out fast." He pointed at Stevens. "Don't do no shooting unless folks shoots at you . . . and keep a-shooting when we come out." He nodded his head. "They's a sidestreet there, and we'll go that way, get off the main drag soon's possible and head into the hills. All right?"

They nodded.

Stevens asked, "What if somebody's hurt?"

"Nobody gets hit," Howie said. He got up. "Git the horses."

# Chapter 25

Aaron Madison and his compatriots, the four senators who had met in Fargo, had decided on a date. Aaron tapped the calendar in his office. The date was two months away, and he was not at all sure he could meet it.

For one thing Ambrose Coyle was constantly nagging him for one thing or another; the man was never satisfied. He needed money, he needed rifles and ammunition—he never had enough—and he needed above all, officers and NCOs. He had been able to train some non coms, but not enough. The people he had to work with were the dregs of humanity. He said it over and over again. They were poor white trash and most of them not worth the powder to blow them to hell.

His message to Aaron was: the armed force could not really be counted on in an emergency.

Aaron bowed his broad shoulders, sighing deeply, head in his hands. So few men could be counted on. It was very possible the armed force would never confront the U.S. Army. If he were politician enough, it might not come to that. He was very aware that the U.S. Armed Forces were at the lowest ebb in the history of the nation—except perhaps for Valley Forge. A strong bluff might be all that was necessary.

It was one of the few things he and Ambrose Coyle agreed on.

But if the bluff did not work . . .

They walked the horses to the bank; the sign read: WAYNE RIVER BANK & TRUST. It was ten-thirty of a bright morning and very few people on the streets.

As they got down, Stevens pulled his rifle from the scabbard and levered a shell into the chamber.

Howie said, "No shooting unless you have to, hear?"

Stevens nodded and watched the three enter the bank. He stood between the horses and eyed the street, his heart slamming against his chest; he could feel it pounding in his ears. He had never figured to be part of a bank-robbing gang!

No one was looking his way. A man came into town on a wagon and went by with never a glance. A few folks farther down the street were gassing and spitting and two old timers came out of a store and sat in tilted-back chairs half a block away. It was very calm and quiet. He took long breaths, remembering that Willie had said it would all be over in a minute.

Then he heard the shots. They came from somewhere inside the bank!

Stevens saw the people on the street turn and look his way. Each one of them frozen for a second or two, then several men ran off the street and someone yelled.

Howie and Willie came running from the bank, each

man had a gray sack in his arms. Howie shouted something and Stevens piled on his horse, wide-eyed. Where was Nate? He had no chance to ask. Howie was off like a shot.

Someone fired at them from down the street, five or six shots whined past. Stevens lay along the horse's back, digging in his spurs. Jesus!

He followed Willie around the corner, heart in his throat, and saw Howie give a quick look over his shoulder. They were through the town in a moment and heading toward the low hills east of town. He glanced back, but no one was coming after them. It would take a bit for them to organize a pursuit.

He heard Willie laughing.

What had happened to Nate?

Howie reined in on the first rise of ground. "You-all all right?"

Stevens nodded. "Where's Nate?"

"He got dead. One of them goddamn bankers pulled a gun."

Howie got down and ran his hands over his mount's flanks. "Make sure you ain't hit. . . ."

They examined the horses and went on. Jesus! Nate was dead! He had been so alive only moments before. . . . And neither Will nor Howie seemed overly concerned. That was probably one of the hazards of the game. Nate had been unlucky.

Stevens found himself shaking his head. A hell of a game. Of course, he was a soldier and might die the same way, except that there was little possibility of a war now. The Big War had passed, settling the fate of the Union, and not likely to be another one soon.

If there was a pursuit they never saw it at all.

• • •

It took forever to get Colonel Harrison's agreement to have a troop at the place selected. A week went by and Jodie reported that he'd been able to get Libby Fillmore to go along with their plan. She would hide in a nearby house till Aaron Madison was in custody.

Jessica would play Libby's part, wearing Libby's clothes with her blond hair covered by a wrap.

Everything was ready—except the cavalry. It did not arrive at the ambush point on the appointed day. Nor the next.

Annoyed, Ki went looking for the troop and found it a day later at the wrong place. The officer, a young lieutenant, argued with him, showing Ki a map, but finally led the troop to the correct spot.

At last everything was ready.

Then Jodie reported that Aaron and several men had left town that morning, heading south. He had no idea where they had gone.

It was a terrible let-down. It had taken a month to get all the elements of the plan together, meshed, and ready to operate. And Aaron had tossed them all into a cocked hat by leaving town.


Aaron was very pleased. Howie and his men had brought back near nineteen thousand dollars and lost only one man. The money was in cash. He would take three thousand of it to General Coyle personally. It would give him a chance to look at the men—and for them to see him. He might even make a speech. . . .

He had his coach brought around, and with Wilbur Dunning and five men as bodyguards, he went to see Ambrose.

The encampment was in the Thor Valley, a remote area far from any habitations. It took hours to make the journey,

166

and Aaron was in a growling mood when they finally arrived.

Ambrose Coyle was not expecting him and had to be sent for. Aaron was shown into a barracks-like building and given coffee. There was a map of the area on the wall, stuck with pins but no indication what they were for. Coyle's office was locked and Aaron paced the floor, chewing a cigar, hands clasped behind his back, till Coyle arrived.

Coyle was in uniform, with two stars on the shoulder straps. The uniform was more tan than brown and was cut in the style of the Union Army. Coyle looked almost majestic in it. He shook hands with Aaron, unlocked the office, and they went inside, closing the door.

He was very pleased to get the money and put it in a desk drawer at once.

Aaron said, "I didn't see any troops as I came in. . . . "

"They're out on maneuvers at the moment. If the wind changes, you'll be able to hear the firing. What can I do for you, Aaron?"

"I merely wanted to see the facilities. Are you as pessimistic as you sounded earlier?"

Ambrose Coyle sighed. "During the war we had men who were soldiers. They were civilians in uniform, but they became damn good soldiers. These men"—he thrust a hand toward the windows—"are nothing like them. I believe these men will run at the first angry shot."

"Can they be replaced? When our plan is in operation, things will get better, will they not?"

"Slowly."

"You must see that they get better. It's your responsibility."

Coyle regarded his visitor with half-closed eyes. "I know my responsibilities, Aaron. *And* my liabilities."

167

"What does that mean?"

"Did you come here to quarrel with me?"

Aaron took a long breath. "Are you patrolling your perimeters?"

"Of course. But there have been no instances of spying. I doubt if anyone knows we're here."

"Good." Aaron rose and stood at the open window a moment. As Ambrose had said, he could hear the far-off popping of corn in a pan. Rifle fire. They had no artillery. His agents had been unable to get their hands on cannon or Gatlings.

He went to the door and turned. He forced a smile. "Au revoir, general."

Ambrose nodded.

They had the first fall rain, a good downpour that lasted an hour and made rushing rivers of dry washes. It caused havoc with the cavalry troop which had come unprepared for such weather. Half the troop had camped in a sandy wash and was routed out at midnight by roiling water.

The theater did no business, and Jodie did not meet with Jessie and Ki, who had camped high and dry under an overhang. Their scheme had come unraveled.

Ki said, "It depended on too many things happening without fail at exactly the right times. And it depended on Aaron Madison acting as we wished he would act—and he did not."

"We'd better go back and meet with the colonel again."

"Yes, I think so."

Jodie met them the next night with the news. "I found out where Madison went. Did you know he's got a private army!?"

"What!"

Ki said, "An *army!?*"

"That's what Johnny said. He's a deserter—I guess you could call him that. Anyway, he slipped away from the camp."

Jessie was startled. "A camp!"

"How do you know this Johnny?" Ki asked.

"He was a spear-carrier in a play we did and—"

"What's a spear-carrier?"

Jodie smiled. "Somebody who's on stage without lines. He wanted to be an actor, but he—well, never mind that. He says that Madison has several hundred men in uniform, training to be soldiers!"

"Where?"

"In a valley south of here. They have barracks and a drill field, a mess hall—and an ex-Union general commanding."

Ki glanced at Jessica. "We've got to see this."

"Yes. How far south, Jodie?"

"I don't know. I suppose the road goes there. . . ."

"Where is Johnny now?"

"Probably on his way home. He left hours ago. He was afraid Madison would have men on his tail."

They left in the morning in a slight drizzle. It was cold, the first tentative fingers of winter creeping across the land. But by midday the overcast had gone and the sun warmed them.

The road they followed had branched from the more traveled trail and led them farther east. In places it disappeared altogether, and they had to pick it up farther ahead. Ki estimated they had come some twenty-five miles when they reached a broad valley where they could see buildings in the distance.

They also came across a well-worn trail that seemed to circle the valley. Ki said, "It's a guard track. They patrol it." He used the binoculars, examining both directions.

169

"Don't see a patrol, but one'll be along. This is a remote area, so they may come by only once an hour."

The binoculars showed them what seemed to be barracks. There were a few men here and there and in the midst of the buildings, a flag on a high pole.

Ki said, "It looks like a small army post all right. . . . "

"Why does Madison need an army?"

Ki grinned at her. "I was about to ask you the same question."

"He already has the local law in his pockets. Is he going to attack Mexico?"

"Maybe. And put himself on the throne as the new Emperor Maximilian."

Jessie shook her head. "I'm no general, but even I know a few hundred men could not conquer Mexico. Jodie's friend said he had two hundred."

Ki put the binocs away. "Maybe he likes parades. At any rate the colonel will be very interested to hear about this."

"Let's go tell him."

# Chapter 26

Things were better—for the moment. Aaron felt as if he were in the eye of the hurricane. Ambrose Coyle had stopped the eternal nagging, and he had met all his payrolls. He also had a letter from two of his senator backers; they would come to Madison two months hence. The other two would stay in the Senate and work for him from there.

It was not a perfect world, but it was improving.

And then he sat at his desk and began to enter the figures, the cash that Howie had brought him, in his private account book. And discovered someone had cut out pages!

He sat frozen for a moment, staring at the open ledger. Who would dare do this!?

Aaron thought back to the half-Japanese man they had captured . . . had he done it? But he had been carefully searched and nothing had been found on his person. Was it likely the man would have hidden the pages here in the house?

But if he hadn't taken them, then who had?

None of the men around him even knew about the ledgers, and if they did what would the knowledge get them?

No, it had to be the Oriental. Somehow he had concealed them from the searchers, but had he gotten away with them to the outside? That was very unlikely. They were probably stuffed into some crack or niche and might never turn up.

That thought began to mollify him somewhat.

But not entirely. He was still grumbling to himself, feeling edgy, when he walked next door to the theater. Maybe a hour or two of entertainment would clear his mind. He took along Charlie and Hank, and Byron Houdek had his usual seats in the fifth row. . . .

Aaron was prepared for the play, with Libby in the leading role, but instead there was a variety show playing. He had forgotten that once a week Houdek put on the variety performance, with act changes from time to time.

The show was a series of what was called skits, and the audience roared at most of them. Aaron sat and glared at the stage for the most part. He had a rudimentary sense of humor at best, and much of the farce was over his head. He was annoyed that Charlie and Hank laughed as heartily as the others.

And then a skit riveted his attention. It was a parody of himself! Those damned actors were making fun of him! And the audience was screaming with laughter!

Jumping up, Aaron pulled a pistol and began firing at the stage, shouting at the actors as they scattered.

The entire house was in turmoil in a moment. One of his shots hit a lantern and hot oil spilled down a drape and in seconds it was afire.

The flames licked up the drape to the ceiling and people

began to fight their way out of the theater. The actors threw sand and water on the fire, and Aaron climbed onto the stage and went across it to the back and out the rear door with the empty pistol in his hand.

The quick action of the actors saved the theater. They yanked down the drapes and put out the fires. The theater filled with smoke and several were trampled in the rush, but the fire was out.

Byron Houdek, in shirt sleeves, surveyed the mess. "How the hell did this start? Who was shooting?"

They told him about Aaron Madison. Someone said, "He yelled that we were making fun of him."

"But the skit had nothing to do with him!"

"He didn't think so."

Houdek shook his head sadly. "The man's crazy—" He waved at them. "Don't tell him I said so!"

No one laughed.

Houdek directed the cleaning up and afterward sat in his office with a bottle on the desk before him. He would be smart to sell out and go somewhere else. Aaron Madison was getting more and more difficult as a neighbor.

He reached for a sheet of foolscap and began to draft a letter to friends in the East. Could they help him get a theater or, lacking that, a job with a good touring company?

He listed eleven names and set about writing to each one.

Jessica and Ki returned to Fort Gillespie and went at once to Colonel Harrison's office. They had released the troop of cavalry; the plan to get Aaron Madison out of his bailiwick had failed because it was too complicated and depended on Madison doing exactly the right thing.

173

The colonel was understanding. "I have come to the conclusion that we will have to send in troops, as I suggested a long time ago."

"But won't he simply evade the troops?"

"Not if I have my way. I intend to request permission from the War Department to round him up. They will undoubtedly hamstring me as much as they can, but I may be able to wriggle enough to get the job done. I still have some friends in high places. If they will give me one more regiment, I am sure it is possible."

Ki said, "Winter is coming on. . . . "

"Yes. It may be politic to wait until spring. We may have another month of good weather, but I'm afraid the plans cannot be pushed through that soon. Things are different now that the war's over. The generals have become politicians again."

Ki said, "There's one other thing, Colonel. . . . "

"What's that?"

"We know there's an informer here in the fort somewhere. If you start making plans for a campaign, no matter how small, he will know and inform Madison."

Colonel Harrison frowned. "Yes. We haven't been able to dig him out. But we'll have to go ahead despite that."

Jessie said, "There's no way he could telegraph news to Madison, is there?"

Harrison shook his head. "Not unless he goes some distance. The telegraph office in Hanover has orders to refuse any wire to Madison, and to notify me that an attempt was made. It won't stop a message, but it'll slow it down."

Jessie asked, "Will Madison fight you with his private army?"

Harrison pulled at his chin. "I suspect the troops are for show. You say the rumor is that an ex-Union Army general is training them. . . . "

174

"Yes."

"That may be, but his men are still civilians at heart. If they are sent against the regular army, they will be routed. Many of my men are in their third or fourth hitch. They are soldiers. The leader of Madison's troops knows it. He will not be foolish enough to face us."

Ki asked, "How long will it take to get a reply from the War Department?"

"That, I cannot tell you. Maybe a week, maybe two months. They take their time. In this case, because I have discussed it with them before, I suspect permission will be grudging, slow, and maybe refused. But I have to try. There is one other aspect of it, you know."

"What?"

"We don't know how many friends Madison has in Congress."

"Is that likely?" Jessie asked. "He's a murderer!"

Harrison smiled. "He is certain to cover that up. And I must remind you that the worst murderers and evil-doers in history had accomplices. If he has friends in Congress, they may act to block whatever plans I present to my superiors."

Aaron sent a message to Ambrose Coyle suggesting a grand parade of the troops on the parade grounds.

Coyle replied that most of the men had been in training only two months or less and were not ready for such a parade. Because if it did not come off well—and he had every reason to believe it would not—then the men would be affected.

Aaron replied that such a reason was an excuse. He ordered General Coyle to plan a grand parade within two weeks. He would attend with other dignitaries.

In two days Coyle came to Madison and confronted

175

Aaron in his office. "This is a ridiculous request! I simply cannot comply!"

Aaron's face reddened. "Why not?"

"Because the men are still largely untrained. Many still cannot or will not march in step. I have told you over and over again I have no junior officers! I have only bumblers!"

"Dammit, Coyle! I am pouring money into your organization and I expect results! How difficult is a parade, for Christ's sake!"

"More difficult than you imagine—for recruits. I warn you, nothing will go right and afterward the men will be so disorganized it may take a month to get them back to the same place they were before your damned parade."

Aaron scowled. "Maybe you're not the man for this. . . ."

Coyle stood up stiffly. "You're a fool, Aaron Madison! And I was stupid to think you could pull this off!" He stalked to the door and yanked it open. "I resign!" He went out and slammed the door.

Aaron stared, mouth open. Then he hurled an inkwell at the door, swearing. . . .

But he jumped up immediately. What had he done! He could not lose Ambrose! The man was indispensible! He ran downstairs and found Coyle getting into a light canvas-topped wagon and grabbed his arm.

"Ambrose—I—I have to apologize. I admit I was wrong. Come back and let's talk about this."

Coyle turned, regarding him gravely. He took a long breath. "Very well, Aaron. We will talk."

They went back upstairs.

Jessica and Paul Nicholson sat in her hotel room; it was late evening. Paul had brought a tray with food and drink, and they had enjoyed a delightful candlelight supper alone.

The supper finished, she had piled the dishes on the tray and put it aside. Paul poured the last of the wine into two glasses. "Are you any closer to bringing Madison to justice?"

"Nothing I say must appear in your newspaper. . . . "

He smiled and held up his hand. "I promise. Not until you tell me I can write the story."

She nodded. "I can tell you it's been a difficult time. A frustrating time. We have evidence, and I believe witnesses will come forward to testify, but at this moment Madison is in no danger of being arrested."

"The government should have moved against him long ago!"

"The government is made up of men. They apparently seldom see eye to eye on anything. And they constantly complain that they are lacking money or manpower. And Colonel Harrison suspects Madison has powerful friends in high places."

Paul sipped the wine. "He is probably right. . . . "

"So we wait."

"What will you do if the people in Washington turn you down? I mean the War Department. . . . "

Jessica sighed. "I don't know." She finished the wine and put the glass on a sideboard, smiling. "Tomorrow is another day. Let's not live it until we finish this one."

He embraced her. "I agree with such sensible sentiments."

She slid her arms about his neck, and in a moment he lifted her onto the bed.

★

# Chapter 27

Aaron Madison pondered the question of the missing ledger pages and could arrive at only one conclusion. Someone wanted them as evidence against him. He had been aware for several years that there was a possibility he could be brought to trial for his crimes. . . .

Of course that possibility was slight as long as he remained strong and wary, taking advantage of the weakness of the federal government. And having the law in his pocket.

But still, there was a glimmer. . . .

He sent for Bayard Cort, the best-known lawyer in the area. Cort was stout, given to black frock coats and an iron spade beard. He wore steel-rimmed spectacles low on his long nose and was fond of teetering on his heels as he delivered orations on the law. He was very partial to the sound of his own voice.

He stood in Aaron's office, one hand grasping a lapel,

as Aaron asked his opinion. "What about double jeopardy, Mr. Cort? Can a man be tried twice for the same offense?"

"Not under our system, sir. It is one of the protections of our good Anglo-Saxon law."

For Aaron it was the right answer. He hired Cort at once and ordered him to arrange for a trial before the local judge, Simon Vance, as soon as Vance could be sobered up. Every crime of which Aaron was accused would be disposed of in a series of trials, and he would be found not guilty in each case.

Aaron said sternly, "Every trial must be entirely legal."

Cort pulled at his beard. "They could probably be challenged, sir, on the grounds that the court was in your pay."

"How could that be proved?"

"By witnesses, of course."

"I rely on you to see that no challenges occur."

Cort shrugged. "The challenges could take years if they are made, and in the meantime, of course, you would be free. There is no way any attorney could prevent someone from filing a suit."

Aaron grunted. But he enjoyed the idea that his own court would try him and exonerate him. Then let the damned government go begging. He would make sure the issues were so clouded and take so long that in the end nothing would be done against him.

And he bragged about what he had done while he was in bed with Libby. He had made himself invulnerable—or he would be as soon as the various matters were brought into court.

He also mentioned the army officer in his pay at Fort Gillespie. Libby was surprised. "An officer?"

"He's a major, yes. Later on he will join Ambrose Coyle's staff."

Libby could hardly wait to meet with Jodie.

179

Jodie sent the information on to Jessica and Ki. In the matter of law, Aaron was putting himself beyond their reach.

Even Colonel Harrison thought so. "He's stealing a march on us. And I don't know what we can do to stop him." He stood with arms behind his back. "In the other matter—there is only one major on the post. Jennings."

"Your adjutant . . ."

"Yes. He is in a position to know everything that occurs, he reads all official mail . . . in short, he is as well informed as I am." He waved a hand. "But leave Jennings to me. I'll get the truth out of him—and take the appropriate steps." He crossed to his desk and picked up a telegraph sheet. "This came last night late. It looks like Aaron Madison is guilty of another bank robbery. The Wayne River Bank was held up and one of the robbers killed. The dead man has been identified as having worked for Madison several years."

Jessie said, "Now that we know he's got a private army, no wonder he needs cash."

They returned to the hotel in Hanover, but the very next morning Colonel Harrison sent for them again. Events were moving swiftly, he said when they appeared in his office.

"The War Department has finally employed an intelligence officer worth his salt." Harrison had a letter in his hand as he faced them. "We knew the names of the senators who met Aaron Madison in Fargo, and now we have discovered his plan."

"What is it?"

"He plans to carve out another state, to be called Madison, with himself as governor . . . and chief tax-gatherer."

Ki smiled. "Chief tax-gatherer!"

"That's the crux of it, yes."

Jessica said, "You mean he would collect millions in taxes — and disappear?"

"That's what we think," Harrison said, nodding. He shook the papers. "The senators, two of them, are on the way here to meet Madison." He turned to the map on the wall. "The nearest train depot is LePine, here." He tapped it with his finger. "From there, the straightest route to Madison runs here. . . . " He traced it. "I will have a company of men intercept the senators at Benton. It's a tiny place, hardly a town at all. With the senators in my custody, I will move on Madison at once."

Jessie asked, "How can you be sure the senators will take that route?"

Harrison smiled. "Our new intelligence officer reads their mail and telegrams . . . and sends them on. I want you two in on the finish of this thing."

"Yes, certainly."

Ki said, "Why don't we meet your men at Benton?"

"Good. I'll inform Captain Riddell."

As the colonel had said, Benton was hardly a town at all. It was a settlement, composed of a store, a saloon, a blacksmith shop, a stable, and a few scattered houses and shacks. There were a dozen corrals, everything covered with a film of dust.

The stable was a weatherbeaten, run-down building that sagged toward the east and they were able to bed down in two of the stalls. The owner, a partially deaf oldster, had a bed in a loft and did his cooking in a smelly back room on a black-belly stove.

They arrived before the soldiers, and had gone to the general store for provisions when the riders appeared. Ki peered through a grimy window as four men rode in. In a moment he hissed at Jessica.

181

She joined him. "What is it?"

"Look! It's Aaron Madison!"

It was indeed. The big man got down wearily in front of the saloon and the three others followed him inside.

Ki snapped his fingers. "He's come to meet his friends! This is an ideal place, no telegraph, a tiny town where he isn't known. . . . "

"So he'll escort them to Madison."

Ki looked at her. "Will he?"

"Of course he's not alone. There're three with him."

Ki frowned at the saloon front across the dusty street. "It would be a mistake to go in there after him. But we don't know how long he'll stay here. Maybe he's meeting his friends somewhere else."

"You just said this is an ideal place."

"Well, *I* think it is. Maybe he doesn't." He drew his revolver, flicked open the loading gate and rolled the cylinder down his arm, looking at the brass.

Jessica said suddenly, "He's coming out of the saloon!"

"We can't let him get away." Ki opened the front door of the store and stepped onto the board porch. She followed, moving to one side.

Ki went down the steps into the street, and Madison saw him at once, staring at him intently, with some surprise, Jessica thought. Madison said something to one of the men with him, and the man turned to look at Ki, then drew his pistol.

Ki said softly, "I see him. . . . "

The man was standing between horses. He jumped into the street in a quick move, his pistol came up, and Ki fired.

Jessica saw dust jump off the man's shirt front. He slumped, fired into the ground, and fell on his face. She watched the youngest of the three circle around the horses.

She pulled the hammer back on the Colt and moved farther from Ki.

Aaron Madison had ducked down with the firing. She saw him crawling behind the horses, and she fired a quick shot at his legs. The bullet nicked a horse and the animal reared—and in the next moment all four horses bunched and ran into the street.

The second man fired where Ki had been, but he was on his stomach, rolling. He fired three times and the man spun away, dropping his gun. Jessica fired at the youngest man at the same time. His bullets smashed the wood of the porch near her . . . then he fell heavily, arms outstretched.

Aaron rose, pointing his pistol at Jessica. She turned, to look into the muzzle. He said, "Drop your gun."

Ki stood, his Colt extended, clicking back the hammer.

Aaron said, "I counted your shots." He glanced an instant at Ki. "Your gun is empty."

Ki tossed the Colt at him and Aaron reacted, throwing up his arm. In that instant Ki hurled a *shuriken*. Aaron fired into the air and staggered, grabbing at his throat. He stared at Ki with terrible, round eyes and fell to his knees . . . then rolled onto his back and blood surrounded his head.

Ki picked up his pistol and slowly began reloading it.

Jessie said, "You only fired four times."

"Yes, but I was never good at arithmetic. He might have been right."

With Aaron Madison's death, his plan collapsed. Colonel Harrison's troops rode into Madison and rounded up Aaron's henchmen to hold for a federal judge. It would take a while for the land that had been under his thumb to settle into peaceful ways . . . but Aaron would soon be forgotten, and nothing would remain of his making.